THE PROMISED LAND DIARIES

4

The
Peaceful
Warrior

The Diary of Deborah's Armor Bearer

Israel

1200 B.C.

Diary One
Bethel

My Home in Bethel

I've just escaped to the roof. The sun rose moments ago over the stone houses and dirt roads. The sky to the east glows with fiery colors, but the hills to our west are still wrapped in shadows. The cocks trumpeted their morning call as our neighbor Senaah hammered on our door for the second morning in a row.

Mama and I hadn't even changed out of our sleeping tunics yet. Papa's eyes sparked with anger. Elam, my fifteen-year-old brother (I'm ten, by the way), put an arm around Papa's sinewy shoulders, and they stepped outside. As soon as they were a few paces away, I crawled to the door on my hands and knees and crept outside. I raced up the stone steps to our roof.

Our roof is flat and wide. It's here that we sleep when the air is hot and stagnant in our house. Bethel is tucked into the southern slope of a rocky hill. I can see many rooftops and narrow winding roads from where I sit now. Far to the south, the walled city of Yerushalayim rests upon its sloping hills.

Papa and Elam are standing in the road now. Roosters and chickens are pecking at the dropped grain scattered in the dust around their sandaled feet. Papa is trying to speak in a hushed voice so he doesn't disturb the rest of the neighbors. Senaah the Thorny (that's what I call him because his name means "thorny") is raising his ugly voice higher and higher. It's the same story as yesterday.

Papa is a tent maker, and Senaah came to him many days ago needing a new goatskin tent. Though he lives in a stone house like ours, he uses his tent when he goes into the fields with the flocks. Sometimes he moves them far away and is gone for a long time. That's when everyone in Bethel is the happiest. Senaah is a thorn in our town.

Papa didn't want to do business with him, but Mama said he had no choice because Senaah is our neighbor. We should treat him like everyone else, she said, because that's what

God would want us to do. Papa gave in, but he did so with great reluctance.

Papa and Senaah agreed on a fair price. Half of it was to be paid up front, and the rest was to be paid when the tent was delivered. The problem arose when Papa delivered the tent two days ago.

Senaah lives four houses away, but I heard every word of their conversation.

"I won't pay a shekel more for this tent, Obadiah," he growled at my father. "Look at this craftsmanship. The skin must have come from a rotten goat, and the stitching isn't even straight."

I winced. I knew right away this wasn't going to be good. Papa's reputation as a tent maker has spread beyond the boundaries of the tribe of Benjamin, where we live. He has made tents for men in the tribe of Manasseh and even the tribe of Asher on the coast of the Great Sea. He has never ever been accused of poor craftsmanship.

I dragged Elam outside that morning so he could hear what was going on. "Do you hear what that . . . that . . . *thorn* is saying?" I cried.

Elam inclined his ear. "He's a thief, Persis," he told me. "Everyone knows that. Papa's tents are the finest anywhere. You watch. Now Senaah says he won't pay another shekel for the tent. Tomorrow or the next day he'll demand to have all of his money returned to him. He's done this to other people in the town who have tried to do business with him."

Papa walked toward us, shaking his head. He'd left the tent with Senaah. I knew he wanted to have words with Mama. I could see it in his eyes, and Mama could too. He was frustrated that he'd allowed her to talk him into doing business with the Thorn. Even so, he didn't say one thing. I've never heard Papa say a cross word to Mama in my whole life.

That was two days ago. Yesterday at daybreak Senaah rapped on our door and demanded that Papa return his silver shekels. Elam was right.

"I'll return your money when you return my tent," Papa told him. His voice was cold and unwavering.

This morning, from what I can tell, it's the same story. Right now I'm watching the toe of Elam's left foot reach back and rub his right ankle. He doesn't know that a horde of biting black ants rages beside his feet. Someone threw out their leftover supper for the wild dogs, and the ants have descended upon it like a shifting, black blanket.

Oh, Papa and Elam are returning to the house now. Senaah shot them an evil look, raised his arm, and shook his fist. The loose sleeve of his robe fell down and revealed his bare arm. The baring of the arm is a very serious gesture. In this case, it means that Senaah intends to stir up trouble.

I'm glad Papa and Elam didn't see it. I watched Senaah turn on his heel and walk away, kicking the loose dirt with his foot. He disappeared in a cloud of brown dust. I have to go downstairs and see what's going on.

First Watch

It's late in the day, and Papa and Elam and I just returned from Mushi's house. When I came downstairs this morning, Mama was encouraging Papa to visit him. Mushi is Papa's closest friend, and he's very wise. He seems to know things that ordinary people don't. Papa thinks God talks to him.

"He's a good friend to you, Obadiah," Mama told him. "I don't know what to do about this incident with Senaah. He won't leave us alone. Go and speak to Mushi and then pray about the whole thing. The Lord will instruct you."

I followed Papa and Elam through the town. Mushi lives on the outskirts because he's a tanner and tanners aren't well thought of. Even though his work is important—he prepares the goatskin for Papa's tents and makes sandals, water and wine skins, and lots of other important things—he still works with dead animals. Anyone who works with dead animals is considered ceremonially unclean.

We walked past the stone houses scattered here and there and past the small shops snuggled against one another like sheep in a pen. Papa bent low and stuck his head into the open door of the bakery. All the doorways in our village are built low so that we have to bend down to pass through them. They're built this way to discourage marauders from entering our homes and businesses. If they can't ride through a doorway on horseback or if our doorways look unattractive, they may think we're very poor and ride on. Sometimes this works, but sometimes it doesn't.

Tabeal the baker was sitting on a mat in the middle of the floor, smoking his pipe. A ring of smoke encircled his head like a smudged wreath. The shelves behind him were dusty and mostly empty.

Bandits had pillaged most of our fields that used to be cultivated for grain. Without the grain, Tabeal couldn't bake his breads and other sweet confections. More and more of the townspeople, our friends, have left. Many of them have fled to the hills and the forests.

Tabeal and Papa exchanged greetings, Papa laughed at something Tabeal said, and we moved past.

The wooden shutters of the potter's shop were closed tight. "Ah, Chuza must be ill again," Papa commented. "I will check on him later." The door to the weaver's shop was open, but we didn't see anyone inside. Iscah had left a long time ago, the very first time his shop was robbed.

We picked our way through rocky outcroppings until a young fig orchard and a freshly planted vineyard appeared on our right. A light breeze told me that Mushi's shop wasn't far way. The odor of rotten meat and rancid blood and guts made my eyes water and my stomach turn.

The putrid smell is another reason Mushi's shop is on the outskirts of town. Tanneries and graves, both associated with the dead and the decaying, can be located on any side of town except the west: The wind usually blows from that direction. No one wants that smell carried on the breeze into their homes.

We Arrive at Mushi's Place

The little shop peeked out from a stony field, and we walked into the courtyard. Rows of lifeless sheepskins were piled in the sawdust. They were tied up tight and bulged with water and oak chips. I knew, from my questions of the past, that these particular skins would be made into leather bottles or water skins.

Two small rooms were on either side of the courtyard, and I peeked into one. This was where Mushi stored the goods he'd made. The room smelled of new leather: strong, slightly bitter, and clean. Deep niches in the walls held belts and leather girdles. Sandals of all sizes were lined up on the floor. Pouches and skins were spread out on mats. Treated hides from sheep, lambs, goats, and cows were piled beside the door within easy reach.

Every time I come to Mushi's shop, I sneak into this room. I like it. It's orderly and neat, and it's always the same. This comforts me. When Mushi sells a water skin, he makes another to replace it. Today, though, something was different. I squinted my eyes and peered at the back wall. It was too dark to see properly, so I stepped inside and walked across the dirt floor.

There were at least forty or fifty, maybe more, small leather shields called "bucklers." Larger shields, but fewer of them, were propped up behind the bucklers. I ran my hand over the soft, smooth leather. On impulse I picked up one of the smaller ones. It was heavier than I'd expected. On the back were two leather handles. I slipped my arm through the top one. It was wider than the bottom one, and the strap rested just below my elbow. My hand fit into the smaller handle at the bottom, and my fingers folded around the leather.

As I held the buckler, I saw Mushi's trademark. The letter *M* was stitched on the back of the shield, at the very bottom above the seam. It stands for "Mushi," and he stitches this letter on everything he makes.

This was the first time I'd ever touched a real shield. I wondered why Mushi was making them and how he was able to make them at all. He doesn't have so many flocks anymore. No one does.

Elam called to me. I saw his head in the doorway, but I knew he couldn't see me clearly in the shadows. I dropped the shield and motioned for him to come inside quickly.

I watched his face when he saw the shields. His brows furrowed, but he didn't say anything. He just took my hand and led me out of the room.

We stepped out of the bright sunshine into the other small room beside the courtyard—the workshop. Mushi was sitting on a stool. His back was hunched over a piece of leather on top of a makeshift table of wide wooden planks. He was engrossed in his work and didn't hear us arrive.

Beams of white light squeezed through two narrow windows near the top of the wall. They illuminated the tiny particles of dust and animal hair that clogged the air. My throat was tight and dry, and my nose began to twitch. I reached up and squeezed my nostrils closed, but it was too late. I let out a monstrous sneeze.

Mushi jumped out of his chair, and a small, sharp knife flew from his hand. It whizzed so close to my head that I saw the metal blade glint in my eyes and felt the rush of air on my cheek. Mushi, Papa, and Elam all stared at me. I wanted to disappear into the dirt beneath my feet—until Mushi began to laugh. His little shoulders shook with such pleasure that even Papa chuckled.

"Persis!" he gasped. He draped his arm around my shoulders. "As I recall, your name means 'one who takes by storm.' Obadiah, mark my words, someday this girl of yours will take more than this small tanner by storm."

I'll have to finish later. Elam just told me Mama is looking for me. It's time to begin the supper preparations.

Twilight

I've returned. Supper was delicious, but it's time to finish my story! Back to the workshop . . .

For the next few hours, Papa, Mushi, and Elam had a spirited discussion. It's always that way when they're together. I walked around the workshop with my scarf pressed against my nose so that I couldn't smell the decay. I pretended to study the skins and tools of Mushi's trade, but I listened to every word that was said.

"Our situation is intolerable," Papa moaned. "Since Ehud died, there has been no order in the land. Corrupt men like Senaah ravage our towns. They're no better than the Canaanites who torment us. Who is our authority? What will become of us?"

Ehud had been a great judge and a hero to our people. He'd ruled the land during the days when the Moabites terrorized us, just like the Canaanites do now. Though he died long before I was born, his legend lives. Papa has told his heroic story to me many times. It always goes like this:

"Eglon was the king of the Moabites, the descendants of Esau who lived east of the Salt Sea. Almost one hundred years after Joshua led our people into the Promised Land, Eglon marched across the Jordan River and conquered part of Israel. He set up his throne in Jericho and demanded that the Israelites pay tribute to him.

"Ehud came up with a clever plan. He made a double-edged sword, hid it on his right thigh, and went to Eglon to deliver the tribute. Since he was left handed, the guards didn't bother to check his right side. He entered the upper room of the king's summer palace and told Eglon, 'I have a secret message for you, O king.' When the king's attendants learned that the message was secret, they left him alone.

"Then Ehud clarified his message. 'I have a message from God for you.' As the king rose from his seat, Ehud reached with his left hand and drew the sword from his right thigh. He plunged it into the king's huge belly, and the handle sank into the flesh after the blade. Three rolls of fat closed over it.

"Ehud rushed to the porch, shut the doors of the upper room behind him, and locked them tight. He fled the palace before anyone realized the king was dead. Once he had returned to Israel, he climbed to the top of the tallest hill of Mount Ephraim and sounded a trumpet. His call echoed through the valley, and the Israelites flew from the hills and gathered around their leader. 'Follow me!' he shouted. 'For the LORD has given Moab, your enemy, into your hands.'

"That day the Israelites struck down ten thousand Moabites; not a single man escaped. For the next eighty years Israel had peace from all of her enemies."

Elam looked Papa squarely in the eye. "Judge Deborah is our authority now. Give her a chance, Papa. It's our fault that our land is in such disarray. When Ehud died, the people turned their backs on God for twenty years. They gave thanks to their idols instead of to the Lord."

Mushi rapped his knuckles on the wooden table. "Your son is very wise, Obadiah. You know it's true. God put Deborah in place for a reason. Like Ehud before her and Othniel before him, Deborah is sure to be our deliverer.

"The Lord has heard our cries. Our oppression has ripened, and it can't be tolerated anymore. The Canaanites occupy the narrow pass from the Valley of Jezreel into the coastal plain north of Haifa now. They control the roads connecting Galilee with the sea and the Jordan Valley to the south. Deborah will act because she has to. If she doesn't, we'll all be dead before long."

Papa snorted. "Perhaps you're right, Mushi, but in the meantime, what is to be done with our neighbor Senaah?"

I tingle even now as I recall Mushi's words to Papa: "You know what you must do, friend," he said. "He's given you no choice. You must take your grievance to Deborah, and she will hear your case. Leave Bethel and walk south in the Valley of Ephraim. It's not far. You'll find her before you reach Ramah. She sits beneath the tallest palm tree. It's called the 'Palm of Deborah.'"

The sky is a deep purple now. One by one the little houses blink yellow with the fire of burning lamp wicks. Many of the villagers are preparing their roofs for slumber. Every night my eyes are drawn toward Yerushalayim. Mushi says that one day it will be a city of peace where God's people will live and worship. Now our enemies, the Jebusites, descendants of the Canaanites, occupy it. Perhaps he's right. Every evening at twilight a crown of stars hangs above those hills.

Mama just warned me that I must unroll my mattress and go to sleep. She said Papa and Elam will leave in the morning to see Deborah. No one knows it yet, but I'm going too. I want to see for myself if she really sits beneath a palm tree. I want to look into the eyes of the woman Mushi believes will deliver our people.

Almost Daybreak

I watched Elam stir from his slumber a short while ago. I've been awake for hours. In the night, he moved his mattress to the roof where mine is. I tried to tell him last evening that he'd be too hot if he slept in the house, but he didn't listen, as usual.

The stars have lost their sparkle in the sky, and I'm already dressed. I never changed out of my clothes from yesterday. I wanted to be ready to leave so that Papa would see that I was prepared and ready for the journey.

I heard him and Elam talk late into the night.

"Deborah will help our people, Papa," Elam said. "I can't explain why I feel this way. I just do. I believe Mushi is right. God sent her to us to be our deliverer."

I heard Papa's footsteps as he walked back and forth. I knew his hands were clenched behind his back. "Elam, I pray that you're right. King Jabin is wicked, and our enemies have never been so close. I fear that we've lost God's protection. As a people, we've alienated ourselves from God, and now I wonder if he hasn't alienated himself from us."

"Well, perhaps he wants us to stand up and fight!" Elam cried. I heard the passion in his voice, and I felt it rise up in me as well. "I'm ready. I'm ready to fight for my God and my people. I'll do whatever I have to do to save the land God promised to us."

I heard a soft handclap, then Mama's hushed voice. "Sshhh. You'll wake up your sister, Elam. I'm quite sure that God doesn't want you to fight at this very moment."

They were quiet then, and I drifted to sleep not long after that. I feel the same way Elam does. I want to *do* something. I want to make a difference. I don't want to just sew and fetch water and sweep. I'm afraid to tell Mama this. I'm afraid I'll hurt her feelings. I know I have a friend in you, diary.

I hear Mama downstairs. I know by the familiar sounds that she's preparing bread for the journey. I'll go and help her, and then I'll figure out a way to tell Papa that I'm going with them.

The Road toward Ramah

I didn't have the courage to talk to Papa after all. I was too afraid that he'd tell me no. I didn't want to hear him tell me that Mama needed me at home.

I went downstairs and helped Mama prepare the fire in the bake oven. I was quiet, and I felt her eyes on me as I moved about our small courtyard. I gathered bits of brush and weeds and a handful of dried manure and pushed it all into the opening in the mud oven. We let the fire burn while the oven heated. Thick plumes of smoke swirled from the small tunnel at the top. The air was hot and smelly, and Mama rolled out the dough as quickly as she could with her nimble hands.

I studied her hands while she worked. They weren't pretty, but they were strong. Her fingers were small, callused, and muscular. They were the hands of a hardworking woman who had rolled out dough for many years. I held mine out in front of me. They're too pretty and soft. I'll never be respected with hands like these.

Mama raked out the fire and tossed the dough cakes into the burning oven until they were browned. I brushed off some of the black ash with my fingers and rolled them into long rolls while they were still warm and pliable.

Then Mama turned to me. "I've already spoken to your father. He's agreed to let you go."

I stared at her in disbelief. "But I never even mentioned to you that I wanted to go, Mama."

She put her head close to mine. "It's all right, Persis," she told me. "You didn't have to. I know you're different. God told me you were special when you were born. There are certain things you must do. Perhaps God is calling you to do these things. Go and see this Deborah and prove to Papa and your brother that you're capable and intelligent. I already know you are, but they'll need more convincing—they're men."

Papa and Elam and I left the house a while later. Just as we rounded the bend, a pack of wild, mangy dogs nearly ran into us. We'd startled one another. Papa picked up a rock and threw it at them. He scattered all but the leader, the biggest one of all. His eyes were fierce and yellow, and his tail moved from side to side like a menacing whip. He turned and sauntered away, but not before he'd bared his teeth and offered a growl so low and evil it seemed to come not from his throat at all but from the depths of his underbelly.

My arms and legs prickled like chicken flesh. Elam took a step toward him, but Papa put his hand on his arm and stopped him.

"Let him be," he told him. "But take heed. They're just like the Canaanites, lying in wait for us. They prowl about our land and create havoc. Their day will come."

At the foot of the hill just south of the village is a spring. It's my favorite spot. It empties into a large pool cut naturally into the rock and worn smooth over many years. We passed a boy leading several goats from the hill to the pasture below. I've seen him here many times, but I couldn't recall his name, and I don't think he remembered mine. We smiled at one another instead.

Papa stopped for a moment and pointed to a higher ridge on the other side of a narrow, deep valley. It was known as the "mountain east of Bethel."

"Father Abraham pitched his tent on that mountain and built an altar to our Lord," he told us.

He moved several steps to his left and pointed out a rounded hill farther east. I could see the charred rubble of a ruined city from where I stood. "That's the fallen city of Ai. Joshua took it not long after the capture of Jericho. There's a deeply carved valley between here and there, not visible from where we stand. Joshua told five thousand of his men to lay in ambush in that valley and wait for his signal. Joshua and the rest of the Israelites lured the king of Ai and his army away from the city.

"Then the Lord told Joshua to hold his javelin high into the air so he could deliver the city into his hands. When the five thousand saw the metal of the javelin gleaming in the sun, they rushed upon the city and captured it with ease."

We walked just two paces and Papa pointed again. "There! That mound you see is a pile of rocks. After the city was taken, the king of Ai was hung on a tree and left there until evening. At sunset Joshua ordered his body to be thrown down at the entrance to the city gate. That mound of rocks was piled over him. It's still his grave."

We resumed our journey in silence, our thoughts all in the same place.

Papa and Elam have been tense since we left Bethel and entered the valley. It's because robbers often ambush travelers on the open roads now. In the days of old, Papa tells me, the robbers would lurk in the dark. They'd wait on less-traveled, winding roads for a chance wayfarer to pass by. Not anymore. Since all law and order has been abandoned, they terrorize travelers everywhere.

"We shouldn't be bothered on this road," Papa said. "It's too close to Deborah. Since she set up her court between Bethel and Ramah, they've stayed away. But it's still important to keep vigilant. Elam, stay alert and walk behind your sister. Persis, you walk behind me and don't stray."

We've decided to rest for a little while. It's hotter on this road than in the hills where we live. The mountains to the east and to the west trap the heat in the smoldering valley. The sun beats on our backs like an angry master. Papa and Elam are eating the rolls of bread we prepared this morning, but I'm not very hungry. I'm too hot to eat. If Mushi is right, we shouldn't be far from Deborah.

At the Palm of Deborah

I can't believe it! I'm sitting less than forty paces from Deborah! It's true. I could move closer if I wanted, but it's so crowded and chaotic I'm afraid I'll be trampled.

As we neared the heart of the valley, we knew we'd arrived. A throng was gathered around a woman beneath a cluster of palms. The sky was a clear, fragile blue, and my insides trembled as Papa took my hand and pulled me through the crowd. All I wanted to do was get closer to Deborah. Elam walked behind us.

Men were gathered in little groups. Some of them were arguing among themselves. Others were silent, watching and waiting with tired, red eyes. Papa says many of them have traveled very far—from the hills, the desert, and the seacoast— just to bring their disputes before Deborah. Camels, donkeys, and mules were scattered about, feasting on the pink and purple heads of the thistle.

We had to step over and around piles of fly-coated dung to the spot where I'm sitting now. Papa says we have to wait until it's our turn, and no one seems to know when that will be. If there's a system here, we're not aware of it.

I love the sound of the palm trees when they rustle in the wind as they are now. Every now and then the crowd parts and I catch a glimpse of Deborah. Her loose purple robes billow about her. Her hair is as tawny as her skin, and it cascades down her back like a waterfall. A diadem, a symbol of her leadership and power, sits upon her head.

We've already waited for over an hour. I feel fortunate that the crowd is silenced every now and then. While the parties plead their cases before Deborah, no one is allowed to speak. It's the same when Deborah gives her judgment. She holds up a sturdy hand, and those closest to her turn around and whisper to those behind them.

They say, "The parties speak," or "Judge Deborah speaks," whichever the case may be. So it goes until the entire crowd is silenced and all eyes are glued to the noble woman beneath the palm tree.

It seems that some have traveled here with no grievance against their neighbor. They just want to see Deborah with their own eyes. Two old men are sitting on a mat not far from me. I'm trying not to eavesdrop, but they're speaking very loudly, and I can't help but hear.

"She's the wife of Lappidoth, you know," said one with a cane and a bent back. "I never thought I'd live to see this day. Imagine that. First a left-handed judge and now a woman."

"Yes. I can't believe it myself," the other replied. His teeth are rotten, and when the breeze blows I can smell the stench of his mouth. "I've come all the way from Beth Shan to see her. A prophet there said she'll be one of the greatest judges in Israel. A deliverer they called her!"

The first man gasped. "Greater than Ehud the left-handed one? Are you sure he said that?"

"I'm sure. They even call her 'a mother in Israel.'"

I heard Papa say that he spotted Senaah in the crowd. He arrived just a few minutes after we did. "He must have followed us," Elam said. "It's just as well. Deborah can hear both sides of the story, and then she can render a fair judgment."

"There's but one judgment to be made if she knows the laws set down by Moses," Papa replied. "From what I've heard so far, she does indeed."

I've been watching the scribe who sits beside Deborah on a small rug. He records every grievance and every judgment. His hand moves with lightening speed across a roll of papyrus. He dips his pen in and out of his black ink pot before I can take a breath.

His inkhorn, which is his pen case, dangles from the belt of his long robe. I watched him open it up. Pens were stuck into narrow slots like swords in their sheaths. He exchanged the pen he was using for a new one in the case.

I strained my neck to see better. There were plain reeds beside the pens. These would be shaped and sharpened into new pens when he needed them. There was a penknife tucked inside the case as well. He also had an additional ink pot with a hinged lid that fastened with a clasp.

I looked down at my old ink pot and battered pen. They paled in comparison to his fine instruments. Oh well. I feel fortunate to have them no matter what shape they're in. I'm not a scribe, after all.

Papa had been gone for a while, mingling in the crowd. He sat down beside me just now and whispered in my ear. "That scribe will be indispensable to our case."

I tried to hide my surprise that he was confiding in me. It's usually Elam he speaks to in this fashion. "How, Papa?"

"A scribe doesn't just record all of these cases on paper," Papa explained. "He's also a 'doctor of the law.' He knows every law and every punishment set down by Moses. Watch now."

Two men approached Deborah. One accused the other of allowing his cattle to graze in his vineyard. "His goats destroyed my vines," the accuser lamented. "They ate every last leaf and every sour grape. It would serve them right if they all got sour stomachs and died."

The other man, a shepherd, hung his head and stared at his sandaled feet. "He's right. They're mine. They did as he said."

I felt sorry for the shepherd, and I watched Deborah to see what would be done. The scribe reached for a scroll from a box beside his feet. He untied the ribbon, unrolled the paper, and ran a gnarled finger down the page. His finger stopped somewhere in the middle, and he held up the scroll for Deborah to see. She nodded and turned to the accused man.

"Do you own a vineyard, shepherd?"

The man nodded solemnly.

"Then your accuser must be paid in kind for the fruit which was eaten by your flock."

The accuser was bold. He spoke up and said, "I'll be without fruit for at least two seasons. He should pay me for two seasons of lost fruit."

Deborah held up her hand. "I too come from a land of vineyards. Your fruit will be lost for just one season, and this is all this man is required to pay you."

She turned back to the shepherd. "Keep your flocks away from his fields. Pay him from the firstfruits of your vineyard the amount of fruit that was lost from his vines. No less and no more."

She glanced at the accuser one more time. "For one season only."

I looked over at Papa and saw his head move up and down. It meant that he was satisfied.

Oh! Deborah has glanced our way. It's time for Papa to present his case.

Back in Bethel—Evening

Justice prevailed today! Deborah ruled in Papa's favor, and Senaah slithered back to Bethel like the snake he is. I was so proud of my father this afternoon. He held his head high and proud and gave Deborah a detailed account of the business transaction between him and Senaah. Elam was the witness, and he testified to its truth.

Senaah was foolish enough to bring Papa's tent. When Deborah ran her fingers over the smooth, black cloth, we all held our breath. She turned it over and examined the tight seams and the small, slanted stitches. Her blue eyes clouded over when she looked at Senaah. His face was screwed up in a scowl, and his eyes were black and beady like little bugs.

"This is a fine tent," she remarked. "In fact, it's one of the finest I've ever seen. Not only did Obadiah son of Benaiah keep his word, he offered you a very fair price. This tent is worth far more than he charged you."

The old scribe beside her cleared his throat and reached into the carved wooden box. He but took out a yellowed scroll, unrolled it, and held it up for Deborah to see. Her eyes moved from right to left as she read the Hebrew script.

"I render my verdict, according to the Word of our Lord as was delivered to Moses. Senaah son of Shuppim, it is my judgment that you cheated your neighbor Obadiah son of Benaiah the wages agreed upon in your business transaction. Therefore, I order you to make restitution in full.

"You will pay the remainder of the monies agreed upon, and you will make an additional payment equaling one fifth of the value of the tent. You shall give it all to Obadiah on the day you present your guilt offering to the Lord. Then God can forgive your sins. Pick a ram from your flock, one without defect or blemish, and present it to the priest. He will make atonement for you before the Lord."

I watched Senaah open his mouth to protest, but he thought twice about it and pursed his lips together.

Deborah looked at Papa. "Obadiah son of Benaiah, you will keep the wages already paid to you by Senaah son of Shuppim, and you will accept additional wages equaling one fifth the value of your tent."

Elam patted Papa on the back, and I heard Senaah grunt behind us. I felt Deborah's eyes float over me, and I looked up. For a brief second our eyes connected, and I thought I saw a smile touch her lips. She moved away then, and her purple robes billowed behind her like wings.

Several Days Have Passed

A terrible thing has just happened, and Papa is angrier than I've ever seen him. I'm afraid he'll kill someone. Mama and I went down to the spring late in the day to draw our water. We held our jugs on our hips and climbed over the stones and rocks until we reached the clear pool. I lowered my jug and was about to dip it into the water, when I heard a noise in the bushes beside me.

A boy was lying on his stomach in the brush! He was the very one I told you about earlier—the one I've seen many times coming and going from the hill to the pasture land. He didn't say a word, but he pointed to the short bluff behind the smooth wall of the pool. An archer stood tall with his bow drawn and his arrow pointed right at my heart. Two more bowmen were aiming at Mama!

The boy whispered, "Back up slowly, and they won't hurt you. They're Canaanites. They're camped nearby, and they're guarding the well. Don't come back until I tell you it's safe."

By this time, Mama had seen the archers as well. I put my hand on her arm and pulled her backward. Without another word, we turned and climbed back up our hill. We left our only jugs at the spring.

Mama ran to tell Papa. She was trembling, and I was happy to see that Papa put his arms around her and held her for a long time. Then he left, and Elam followed him down the hill. His eyes were red, and the blue vein in his neck pulsed so that I could count the beats of his heart.

I can't stop thinking about the boy beneath the bush. What was he doing there? My gratitude to him is beyond measure. I believe that had he not warned me, Mama and I would be lying dead by the spring, our hearts pierced and our bodies bloodied. We were so busy chatting together that we were oblivious to the danger at hand.

Papa has been gone for quite some time. If he and Elam don't return soon, I'll have to sneak away to see what has happened.

Much Later

As it turned out, I did sneak away. One of the women of the town heard the news and called on Mama. When they became engrossed in their conversation, I left. I thought it unwise to take the same path down the mountain, so I moved east instead and headed toward the hill's edge. I climbed down the narrow slope and slipped on the loose rocks, scratching my hands and elbows.

When I'd descended quite a ways into the valley, I began my ascent up the western face. This side was steeper and harder to climb, and I had to move with care so I wouldn't fall. When I neared the top, I heard voices. I didn't climb over, but I peeked my head over the top.

Three Canaanites were gathered in a clearing. The spring was too far away to see, but I knew they were the archers from the pool. Their quivers were still slung over their shoulders, and their long bows were propped up against a rock. A pile of dried wood was in the center of a circle of rocks, and three dead quail were thrown to the side. They had set up camp, so I knew they'd be in Bethel for at least a little while.

I slipped back down the slope quiet as a fox at night and returned home. When I arrived, Papa and Elam had just returned.

"They were gone by the time we got there," Elam was telling Mama. "Maybe they got their water and left."

"We can't be sure," Papa said to Mama. "I don't want you or Persis to go near the spring until we're sure it's safe. We found the jugs you left and filled them. We should have enough water to last several days if we're careful. We'll decide what to do after that."

Papa and Mama are in the courtyard now. Their voices are hushed, so I know I'm not supposed to hear their conversation. I did hear one snippet though. Papa said it's strange that the Canaanites would come to Bethel to gather water from the spring.

"They have a spring inside the walls of Yerushalayim," he said. "A pipe runs underground from that spring to the heart of the city. They have no reason to use our water. I have to believe they're just intent upon terrorizing us now. There's no telling what lies ahead for us."

Papa has advised us to sleep indoors tonight. I've spread my mattress on the raised platform that runs along the sides of the walls, and I'm sitting on it. Elam is already reclining on his. I can tell he isn't asleep even though his eyes are closed. His thumb is tap-tap-tapping on his stomach.

"Elam!" I whispered a few minutes ago.

"What?" he mumbled.

"The Canaanites haven't left yet. They've set up camp about an acre from the spring."

His eyes flew open and then he sat up. "How do you know?" he asked. He glanced over his shoulder toward the courtyard. "You snuck away after we left, didn't you?"

I nodded.

"Which way did you go?"

"East toward the edge of the hill, then into the valley. I climbed up the western slope."

"All right," he told me. "I'll figure out a way to tell Papa without his knowing it was you who discovered this."

Elam was silent for quite a while, and I waited for him to rebuke me. He surprised me with what he said next. "You're a brave girl, Persis. But then again, you've always been different. You're not a typical girl. I like that." He messed up my wavy red hair with his big hand and lay back down on his mattress.

The dogs are howling tonight, and it sounds like they're right outside our house. Mama and Papa have just come in, and Papa bolted the door. It's been a spooky day, and it's a spooky night. I'll be glad when morning arrives.

Early Morning

I awoke to voices in the street. Mama was standing at the open door. The sunshine poured into the room and made it hot. I stood beside her and rested my arm around her waist. Papa and Elam were gathered outside with a group of men. There was Mushi, Tabeal the baker, Chuza the potter, who had recovered from his illness, and two other men I recognized but whose names I didn't know.

"What's going on?" I asked her.

She shook her head, and I saw sadness in her pretty face. Little lines have always creased the fragile skin beneath her eyes, but in the last few months there are more of them.

"It doesn't look good, Persis," she told me. "There's word that the traders refuse to drive their caravans to this part of the country. The banditti have ambushed them too many times. Without the caravans, we'll suffer. As it is, our crops are ruined and our resources are running low."

My heart beat fast in response to her words. "I don't understand," I cried. "Didn't God promise this land to us? Why did we come here if it was going to be like this? Why is God taking everything away from us?"

"Persis!" Mama's voice was sharp, and it cut into me. "Don't ever blame God. He isn't taking our land. We did this to ourselves when our people turned our backs on him. Now he has turned his back on us. We must cry out for mercy and forgiveness. He'll hear our cries. He'll rescue us. We must be faithful."

Later

The men have finally left. I thought they'd never go away. All day they discussed and debated the condition of our country. They sat in our courtyard with Papa for a long time. Mama said we had to fix them something to eat, so we did.

They sat on the rooftop. They went back into the street. They talked of endless solutions, but in the end they agreed that without God's divine intervention, our cause is a hopeless one. The Canaanites outnumber our people. They have iron beasts called chariots, which are pulled by giant horses. Soldiers in armor stand in the chariots with bows and arrows, spears, javelins, and lances.

Our weapons are few, and many of those are rusted with age and disuse. I'm trying not to feel down. Mama is right. God will hear our cries. I prayed just a short while ago and asked the Lord again to save us. I also asked him to use me. I can't tell anyone about my prayer because I'm afraid they'll laugh. "Oh, Persis wants to take the world by storm again!" How many times I have heard that? I can't even remember.

The Thorn Is Back

There was a rumor in town that Senaah the Thorny had returned from the fields. We found out today that the rumor is true. Just past sunrise, I heard a rustling outside the house near the courtyard. I saw a shadow creep past the door. There's a slight crack between the stone wall and the wooden door. It was through this crack that I glimpsed a dark figure.

Elam saw it too, and he waited a few moments before he opened the door. A small pouch filled with silver shekels was sitting on the stoop. When we brought it to Papa, he counted it and said it must be from Senaah. It was the money Deborah ordered him to pay for the tent.

No one was relieved or happy though. Papa tried to hide it, but Elam saw a talisman of a Canaanite god inside the bag. He said it was a carved figure of Asherah. She's the goddess of war and the sister of Baal, the chief god of the Canaanites.

The New Moon Has Risen

The crescent new moon is beautiful in the night sky! Mama and Papa call it the "first visible sliver." This means a new month is upon us. A priest from the tribe of Levi has lit a fire on the hill beside us. It can be seen for many acres. When the people in the surrounding towns see the first flames, they know the new month has been sanctified. Then they light their own fires on the hilltops. Now flames burn like torches in the black sky, and the blasts of trumpets echo from hill to hill.

Tomorrow is New Moon Day, and I'm grateful it's a day of complete rest. We aren't allowed to do any chores. Papa and Elam will go to the priest to make a burnt offering, a grain offering, and a sin offering to the Lord. When they return, we'll feast upon roasted lamb, stewed quail with rice and gravy, porridge made with corn, and honey donuts.

It's true that our supplies are running low. Last year we ate juicy fruit from the trees. This year the trees are barren. All our fruit was stolen in the night. Oh well. It's not a time to complain. It's a time to be grateful. The dawn of the New Moon Day is almost upon us.

Two Days Later—the Middle of the Night

I must write fast. A short time ago, we were startled from our sleep again. Someone was rapping on our doorpost. There were shouts in the street, and the dogs were barking like mad. Papa swung open the door, and Mushi charged in. He was breathless, and his hand was on his heart. Mama pulled him over to the ledge where our mattresses were still spread. Droplets of sweat dripped down the sides of his face, and he couldn't speak for several moments.

"I have bad news," he panted. "The Canaanites have raised a large army. They're preparing to attack. I don't know when, but I've heard that a huge force of chariots is assembled at Harosheth Haggoyim in the lee of Mount Carmel."

Papa sank into the cushions beside him and rubbed his forehead up and down with his fingers. Mama was frightened.

"How do you know this?" Papa asked.

"Zephi," Mushi replied.

"Zephi?" Elam repeated with wide eyes. "The boy who lives down the hill?"

Mushi nodded. "He's a spy for Deborah. He's been reporting on the movements of the Canaanites for many moons now."

Papa looked at me. "Did you know this, Persis?"

I shook my head. "No. But this must be the boy who was hiding under the bush when Mama and I went to draw water. He saved our lives. I never knew his name until now."

I still can't believe it as I write this. Zephi, the boy down the hill, is a spy? He can't be that much older than me!

Mushi told us that the Canaanites were waiting for Sisera, the commander of their army, to give orders to move ahead. Until he did, they were camped beneath the shadow of the mountain.

"Does Deborah know this?" Papa said.

"Zephi has left to bring word to her. We'll know more when he returns this evening."

Once again the men are gathered outside, discussing the situation at hand. Mama and I are sitting inside, watching and waiting.

Zephi Returns

He rode into town on his donkey, and the men crowded around him. His water skin was dry, and Mama ordered me to bring him a new skin filled with fresh water. I pushed through the men and held it up to him.

"So now you know," he said with a smile. He drank the water so fast it spilled down his chin and soaked the front of his shirt.

"What news have you for us?" one of the men shouted.

Zephi cleared his throat and sat up straighter on the animal's back. "Deborah is organizing troops as we speak. She's planning to send for Barak son of Abinoam from Kedesh-naphtali. When he arrives, she'll ask him to lead our people to war against the Canaanites. We're in need of men. She wants strong men who are willing to fight for their country."

Elam stepped forward at once. "I'll fight for my country," he said without hesitation.

I looked at Papa. A smile was on his lips, and his eyes were lit with pride. Several more of our young men stepped forward. Mama was standing beside me. "It's not fair," I told her. "I want to help too. I want to do something."

"You *will* do something, Persis," she told me. "You'll stay with me and we'll watch over things while the men are away. This is very important."

I can't sleep, so I'm on the roof. The entire town is lit when the houses are normally black. All the townspeople are disturbed about the news.

When Mushi came in this morning and told us about the Canaanites, I thought of the talisman that was in the pouch of coins Senaah left for Papa. I could tell Elam thought of it too, because he looked at me in a funny way. I could see the remembrance in his eyes. He'd said he was sure it was a charm of Asherah, the Canaanite goddess of war.

Did this mean Senaah knew we were going to war? Elam said he couldn't have known unless he was aligned with our enemies. This is a scary thought. Have we had a traitor living among us all this time? Elam said Senaah's more Canaanite than Hebrew, and he wouldn't be surprised if he took up the sword against his own people.

My brother and many of the men will leave at dawn to join the army. They'll meet at the Palm of Deborah. I've wrestled with my heart all evening, and I've made a decision. I'll go as well. I regret that I can't tell Mama, Papa, and Elam, but I fear they'd never allow it.

As soon as everyone is asleep, I'll go to Zephi and beg him to accompany me through the valley to Deborah. I'll plead my case to her and offer my services. I have to do this. I want to serve God and my country. I won't leave until Zephi agrees to take me.

Into the Night

I waited until I heard Elam's snores. Why did he have to pick tonight to sleep on the roof? Earlier in the evening, I stored a bag with bread and nuts and dates. I also filled a water skin and hid everything behind several tall baskets.

I crept down the stairs with my bag and my skin and walked down the hill with the light of the moon to guide my footsteps. I didn't know where Zephi lived, but I had an idea. I'd always seen him in the area of two or three houses on the middle portion of the hill, so I walked in that direction.

The dirt road took me to the homes I was after, and I knew right away which one be-longed to our spy. It was the only one still inhabited. The others beside it were dark and vacant. The doors were open, and they swung on their metal hinges in the warm wind.

I didn't know what I should do, so I tapped on the doorpost. It opened, and Zephi's head peeked around the frame. His eyebrows lifted in surprise. "Persis!"

I was surprised too. "How do you know my name?" I asked him.

"I know everyone's names. It's my business to know."

He stepped outside, but before he did I tried to look past the door into his house. "Where are your mother and father?" I inquired.

He shook his head. "I have none. My grandfather raised me. He's away most of the time now, so I'm on my own."

I took a deep breath. "Zephi, I want to serve my country, and I need you to take me to Deborah."

He was quiet for several minutes. "All right then," he said at last.

"I won't leave until you agree to take me."

"I figured you wouldn't. I said all right."

"Zephi, this is the most important thing I've ever done," I told him. "I know I'm a girl, but Deborah is a woman, after all."

"Persis! I said all right!"

It was my turn to be quiet. "You did?"

"Yes, but with two conditions. First, you must cut your hair. You'll need to blend in as much as possible and not draw attention to yourself. Not everyone will take kindly to a girl away from home. No matter that Deborah is a woman. She's a judge and a commander. You're not."

I reached back and fingered my long red braid. I'd had long hair since I was a little girl. I let out a little sigh, and Zephi stared at me hard.

"Are you sure you're ready for this?"

I nodded.

"All right then," he answered. "The second condition is that you'll return home at once."

"What?" I cried.

"Sshhh," he whispered and put his hand over my mouth. He backed into the house, and I watched him blow out the flame of his lamp. Thin clouds passed above us and veiled the moon. I blinked my eyes and tried to adjust to the dim light.

Zephi leaned close to my ear. "Persis, it's imperative that you be quiet about all of this.

You must speak of it to no one. There are traitors among us, as you now know. Perhaps they lurk in the bushes as we speak. All of our lives are in jeopardy now. We must pray for God's protection and his guidance."

Zephi made me promise to return home and do something very important. He said it was a ritual that soldiers had practiced for many centuries. It would keep me safe if I found myself on the battlefield.

He walked with me up the hill. "You must fast for three days," he said in a hushed voice. "Then take an unmarked, fresh piece of hide. Dip your pen into the blood of an unblemished white dove and the blood of a calf. Write down your name, your father's name, your mother's name, and the characters of the alphabet.

"When you have done all of this, tuck the hide into your pocket and keep it with you always. No harm will ever befall you if you follow my instructions."

Zephi disappeared when I reached the top of the hill. I turned to reply, but he'd vanished. I heard the wild dogs snarling in the streets over a scrap of rotten food.

I returned home and crept back up the stairs, disappointed that I had to stay for three more days but determined to do what Zephi asked. When I reached the top step, Elam was staring right at me. He was wide awake!

I can barely keep my eyes open, so I must stop for now. I'll finish my story in the morning.

At First Light

My brother has surprised me again. When I returned last night and found him awake, I braced myself to be rebuked.

I waited on the top stair, afraid to breathe.

Elam sat up on his mattress and patted the space beside him.

"Come here, Persis."

I sat beside him, still afraid. He reached behind me and pulled out my bag of provisions and my water skin. He studied them in silence.

"Not leaving for battle just yet?" he asked me. His voice was gentle. It wasn't what I'd expected.

I looked down at my feet. "How did you find out?"

"I was awake when you left. I followed you to Zephi's house and hid in the bushes."

I couldn't believe it. "That was you? Zephi heard a noise in the dark, but we thought it might be Senaah."

Then Elam said the kindest words imaginable. "Persis, I was so proud of you, prouder than I've ever been. I'll leave in the morning because it's what's expected of me. I'd rather die than not fight for God and my country, but it's still an ordinary thing for men like me to do.

"You, on the other hand, are doing the unexpected. You have no example to follow. I believe you're being led by God, and I'll do whatever I can to help you."

He reached behind him and lifted up a blanket. A long spear with a shiny silver head lay on the gray, stone roof. I was too surprised to speak. I reached down and rubbed my fingers over the long, smooth handle.

"Where did you get this?" I asked him.

"I found it." He pointed in the direction of Ai, the fallen city on the hilltop. "There in the rubble and the ruins."

He touched the sharp metal head. "You won't find one like this among our people," he said. "It's made of iron, which means it belonged to a Canaanite. It's far superior to what we'll fight with. Whatever weapons are left in our country are made of bronze or copper. They're softer and rust easily."

I asked Elam if he would take it with him, but he shocked me with his reply.

"No. I want you to take it with you when you go. Present it to Deborah. She's our leader. If God is willing, she'll carry it."

My brother left a few moments ago with many of the men from the town. Mama packed as many provisions for him as he could carry. Then she hugged him tight and sobbed. Papa shook his hand and patted his back, and I saw that his eyes were moist.

Elam made me promise to write a note to Mama and Papa and tell them of my whereabouts before I left. I agreed.

"You're in the Lord's care now, little sister," he told me. "He has put a divine mission before you. Be brave and remember that you're not alone. Hopefully, I'll see you once you reach the camp at Ephraim." He kissed my cheek and walked with the men on the crooked dirt path down the hill.

I scrambled to the rooftop so I could watch him leave. He turned to me and waved. The sun was red over the rubble of Ai. I thought of the king who was hung on the tree and buried beneath the mound of rocks. I pray that we'll be as victorious as Joshua so our leader will be spared the fate of that king.

Later

I've returned from Mushi's shop. It was the first time I've gone there by myself, and I felt strange without Elam and Papa. Mushi was the only one I knew who could help me do what Zephi had instructed me to do. The problem was that I had no idea how to explain why I needed a small piece of hide and the blood of a dove and a calf.

As it turns out, he didn't ask any questions. He looked at me in a peculiar way, nodded his head, and told me to return tomorrow morning. So I will.

The Next Day

It's hard to wait out the days until I can leave. I agreed to fast for three days, but my stomach doesn't understand, and it grumbles continuously. I served our supper tonight, as usual, on a low stand in the middle of the rug. The aroma of the bread and the porridge beneath my nose made me faint with hunger. I thought my saliva would dribble down my chin. Still, I feigned an upset stomach. Mama and Papa looked at me in a strange way, but they said nothing, like Mushi.

I wonder if they know something, but that's unlikely. They're just preoccupied right now. They're worried for Elam and worried for our country. Their thoughts are divided in many directions, and I don't think they notice my strange comings and goings or my peculiar behavior.

Mushi gave me a beautiful piece of hide and a skin of blood. I took it away from the shop and found a quiet place beneath a stand of trees. I dipped my pen into the dark, thick fluid and wrote my name and that of my mother and father. Then I wrote the characters of the alphabet. It still seems like an odd thing to do, but I gave my word.

The blood was bright and ruby red when it touched the skin, but it dried black within minutes. I tucked the hide into the pocket of my tunic and buried the remainder of the blood

beneath the tree. I didn't know what else to do
with it.

Two Days Later—Nightfall

I'll be leaving in a moment. Oh, the feelings that
have erupted within me! The brave girl Elam
left behind has vanished like a ghost. I'm frightened. A pile of red wavy hair sits at my feet, and
I don't have the courage to sweep it away. My
neck is naked without my long hair to cover it,
and now I feel vulnerable and exposed. As if my
hair ever protected me!

As I cut it, the metal of my knife shimmered
in the light of my clay lamp. My hair reminded
me of blood, and the knife became a sword in
the hand of our enemies. I feel chilled to the
bone though the night air is warm.

My water skin and my pouch of food are
hidden with Elam's spear. I've written a letter to
Mama and Papa and left it beneath a rock on the
roof. There's nothing left to be done. I'll take

my diary with me and write again the first chance I have. I'm not sure when that will be.

I must leave now for Zephi's house. Lord, please calm my fears. Help me to remember that you are with me always. I am not alone . . . I am not alone . . .

Diary Two

The Valley of Ephraim

I've Arrived at the Camp

Zephi and I arrived at the court of Deborah several hours ago. There are several tents set up now, and Deborah has been inside one of them since we got here. If I thought it was chaotic the last time I was here with Papa and Elam, I was mistaken. Men are running everywhere, some whispering and some shouting. A courier on horseback just thundered north. He flew like the wind, his cloak sailing behind him.

Zephi was allowed entrance into Deborah's tent. He returned to tell me that the messenger was sent to Kedesh to summon Barak. She'll officially ask him to lead the Israelites to war against the Canaanites.

I haven't spotted Elam yet, but I'm sure I will. All the men from the adjacent villages who volunteered their services are camped here. They're awaiting their orders. I'm sitting in a shady spot now, and my spear rests across my lap. I gripped it in my hand for so many hours that my fingers are numb. I'm afraid to let it out of my sight. Several rough-looking men have looked at it with hungry eyes.

They eye me too as if they're not sure whether I'm a boy or a girl. My hair is short and plain now. It's not a style that women wear. Also, Zephi made me change into a plain white tunic, common among men. Now I'm grateful that he did. I don't want to draw undue attention to myself, although I appear to be doing so anyway.

At Camp Almost a Week Now

I found Elam at last! I was so grateful to see his sweet, familiar face, and I could tell that he was happy to see me too. The camp is spread out over several acres now, so it isn't so easy to find someone. His presence reminded me of my home and of Mama and Papa, and I was overcome with a wave of sadness.

Then I told myself that the reason we're all here is to fight for our country and our freedom so that our families and our homes can be safe. I still miss them, but it helps when I remind myself that I'm here for a greater cause.

I was talking with Elam when two beautiful white donkeys sauntered through the camp. I've never seen such animals. Their coats are pure white. A tall man was riding on one, flanked on either side by footmen. I watched in amazement while the camp parted to make room for them.

Zephi appeared out of nowhere. He's been up and down, back and forth like a worker ant, and I can't keep track of his whereabouts. He appears and disappears without a word or a sound. I suppose this quality is what makes him such a good spy.

"It's Barak," he said. "He's come here to ask Deborah to grant him the power to use force. He can do nothing without her wisdom and authority, and she's weak without the physical force he can muster. One is the head and the other the hands. In order for God to deliver us from our enemy, they must work together."

He took one step away and then turned back. "Be prepared to leave at any time."

Elam noticed that I still held my spear. "You haven't met with Deborah yet?" he asked.

I shook my head. "Not yet, but Zephi keeps telling me that I will soon."

Elam hugged me tight, and then he disappeared into the crowd. I hope I'll see him again soon. He comforts me and helps me feel that I'm not alone. Zephi is a wonderful friend, but no one can take the place of family!

Dusk

I'm resting on my cloak not far from Deborah's tent. I feel the heat of the torch that's dug deep into the dirt beside me. I'm grateful for the light it provides so that I can write. Flames shoot from these long wooden poles throughout the camp.

A lamp blazes inside the tent where Deborah is meeting with Barak. I can see their silhouettes through the cloth walls. They're kneeling on a rug bent over what I imagine to be a map, though I can't be sure.

I shouldn't listen, but their words are carried to me on the night air. I picked up my things and moved farther back, but I can still hear.

"Deborah!" cried Barak a moment ago. "A spark of fire burns within my breast. Grant to me the broad seal of heaven that I might employ whatever means necessary to fight Sisera and his men. We are on the brink of destruction."

I waited for Deborah to reply, and when she did her words vibrated within me.

"My friend," she said, "has not the Lord, the God of Israel, already commanded it? Yes, certainly he has. Take my word for it. He has already whispered in your ear that he desires to use you as an instrument to save Israel.

"He commands you: 'Go, take with you ten thousand men of Naphtali and Zebulun and lead the way to Mount Tabor.'"

"Deborah, "Barak interrupted, "I have one concern, and it troubles me. How can we be assured that Sisera will engage in battle? Once he sees that we have gathered our forces, he may decline to fight. He knows full well that what

God's people lack in weapons, we possess in courage. When we choose to stand against our enemies, we don't often fail."

"I will lure Sisera, the commander of Jabin's army, with his chariots and his troops to the Kishon River. There, through the power and grace of our Lord, I will deliver him into your hands," Deborah replied with calm.

Barak was quiet for a long moment, and at first I thought he didn't intend to reply at all. When he did, I found his words to be extraordinary. "If you go with me, I will go; but if you don't go with me, I won't go."

I heard Deborah sigh. "Very well. I will go with you. But because of the way you are going about this, the honor will not be yours, for the LORD will hand Sisera over to a woman.

"I give you my assurances, Barak. The outcome will be determined in one battle and will not take long at that. You know that your foe Sisera is a celebrated general. He is bold and experienced. He has iron chariots and a multitude of soldiers at his disposal. You must furnish yourself with strength and resolution."

Barak left Deborah's tent just now and went into another. I'm sure it's where he'll sleep while he's in the camp. The white donkeys are grazing in the grass with the common ones just beyond the tents. Their whiteness gives them a ghostly appearance. The other donkeys are watching them. Is it my imagination or do they sense the white donkeys' beauty and their special place in the camp as well? Only important people ride animals as rare as these. I want to touch them and pet their soft muzzles, but I don't dare.

Zephi went into the tent after Barak left. He's standing in the entrance, one foot out and one foot in. Now he's motioning to me with his hand. Oh my. I believe I'm being summoned to meet with Deborah. Calm me, Lord. Please fill my mouth with your words. I must go.

An Hour Later

My hands tremble still. I have to stop every moment or so to calm myself. I want to record my meeting with Deborah in detail, but I may not be able to write at all if I don't stop shaking.

I entered her tent after Zephi motioned to me. She was sitting on a rug studying—yes, I was right—several maps. Her long hair was loose. It cascaded down her back in long waves just like it had the first time I saw her. Without thinking, I reached for my own cropped curls.

I gripped my spear in both hands, and when she turned toward me, I held it out to her. I thought I wouldn't be able to speak.

I don't how to describe her except to say that she's extraordinary. I have seen women more beautiful then Deborah but none so beautiful and intelligent and strong all at once. Her eyes moved over me, and I knew that she captured every detail in one swift look. She's wise and intuitive. I felt it. I knew that I was in the presence of a great leader.

Deborah looked at my spear, and her eyes rested upon the iron head. She reached out and took it from my hands. "Have you come to offer this to me?" she asked with a smile.

"Yes. I would like for you to have it. It's fitting that our leader possess a weapon equal to that of our enemy." I didn't recognize my own voice. It was strong and full of confidence.

She didn't take her eyes from my face. "I don't have an iron weapon," she admitted. "Just one or two made of bronze, and they're weak with age."

"I was told that might be the case," I told her.

"Have you come for any other reason?" she inquired.

"Yes," I replied. My voice was calm though I was not. "I would like to offer my services to you. I'm prepared to serve in any capacity that is needed."

"You are prepared to be a woman among many men?"

"I am."

"God chooses unlikely leaders, Persis. But those who lead must also be willing to serve. I serve at the pleasure of my Lord, and he has called me to be a servant to my people. I will march into battle with those brave souls willing to fight for their country. Since you bear my weapon, it is fitting that you should carry it into battle for me."

I thought that I might faint right then and there. I still think I might faint now. How has this all come about? In a span of a few short moments, she humbled me and taught me that leadership is all about service—to God, to others, and to my country.

In the next moment, she exalted me beyond measure by appointing me her armor bearer.

I turned to leave, but her voice caused me to turn toward her again. "Don't think I don't remember you, Persis, brave daughter of Obadiah. I've waited for you to return. God called you long before you were born, and he has been training you all these years. It's time to pick up your weapons and serve him."

I'm dizzy with delight and gratitude, and I've been moved to tears. The campfires burn, and the flames spark orange and yellow. Glowing red embers drift into the black sky, soaring higher and higher until my eyes are lifted toward heaven. "God has called you," she said. I'll never forget those words, and none will mean more to me.

God is preparing our people for battle now. I can feel it. The preparation begins in our souls. The men are singing Hebrew hymns that I remember from my childhood. Their voices are raised, and they're singing with every breath of their being. Their music is beautiful to me, and I know that it's beautiful to God.

Slumber Must Wait

How will sleep come to me when the camp stirs? Some of the men are sleeping, but many of them are huddled in groups, whispering their thoughts. Elam and Zephi came to me as I was putting down my pen earlier. Zephi had told my brother the news about my meeting with Deborah, and Elam picked me up and swung me around. It was no easy feat for him, I'm sure. I'm not so little anymore.

We fell into deep, quiet thought, but after a time I could stand the silence between us no longer. I needed the cheer and comfort of conversation. Also, there was one thing that had been troubling me.

"I heard Barak say that he wouldn't go into battle if Deborah didn't accompany him." I glanced at both Elam and Zephi. "I don't understand why."

Elam was quick to answer. "It may be because Deborah is a prophetess. He feels that her presence in battle will ensure God's presence as well. He doesn't need her might. He needs her there to direct him and pray for him. He needs her godly counsel."

"Yes, I agree with your brother," Zephi said. "It's like what I told you earlier. Barak can do nothing without Deborah's head, and Deborah is useless in battle without Barak's hands. Their unity is necessary to accomplish what God has called them do."

Zephi and Elam left me then and told me to sleep. Easier said than done! There's a good chance we'll leave sometime tomorrow. I'm going into battle. Those words look strange to me as I read them on my paper. Have I become a soldier?

Morning Has Broken

The arrival of the morning sun brought an unexpected announcement. The men gathered here in the Valley of Ephraim won't travel north with Deborah and Barak after all. They'll stay here and wait on the northern slopes of Mount Ephraim—the chain of hills that borders the valley.

Deborah met again with Barak while the moon was still bright. Zephi said it was decided that the men should wait for a little while. When the time is right, they'll advance north.

In the meantime, Deborah and Barak (and me, of course) will travel north to Kedesh-naphtali.

It's about a three-day journey. We'll wait there while Barak assembles no less than ten thousand men from the nearby tribes. When the troops have been assembled, we'll move southwest toward the slopes of Mount Tabor. Then Sisera will be lured toward the area of the Kishon River in the Valley of Jezreel.

From what I understand, I'll leave with Deborah and Barak in just a few hours. Elam will stay with the troops here and wait for the signal to move forward. It will be at least five days but maybe more.

Zephi is leaving now. He'll travel north and try to get advance word of Sisera's movements. He said there are several observation posts between Mount Ephraim and Mount Tabor. One is on Mount Gilboa on the southern side of the Valley of Jezreel. Another is on the opposite side of the valley on the hill of Moreh. Both posts offer a clear view of both Mount Tabor and Sisera's base camp at Harosheth Haggoyim.

He left just now as I'm writing to you, diary. I watched him ride off on his donkey. Elam excused himself to speak to the men in the camp. It seems he's already taken a position of leadership among the soldiers. That doesn't surprise me! He has a take-charge attitude, but his kindness and honesty make him trustworthy. The men look up to him because of these qualities.

I feel very alone now, and I'll admit a secret to you: I'm frightened and I'm having my doubts. Who am I to serve Deborah as her armor bearer? I have no experience whatsoever. What if I'm a hindrance to her? I suppose time will tell, but I hope it tells before I make a terrible mistake and harm others or myself because of my ignorance.

Later

A boy walked by me a short while ago. I was sure I recognized him! I searched my memory until it came to me. He's from Bethel! He doesn't live far from me, though I've never met him.

I watched him walk north away from the camp. He was either anxious to go to battle and was getting an early start or he was returning home. I decided the latter was the more plausible explanation, and I quickly jotted a note. Perhaps he could take it to Mama and Papa for me. I decided it wouldn't hurt to try.

Dear Mama and Papa,

Of course you read my note and know that I'm in the Valley of Ephraim with Elam. I'm sorry I couldn't tell you myself. I was afraid you wouldn't let me go. Please don't be angry with me, and don't worry about me either! Deborah has appointed me to be her armor bearer! I thought you'd be proud to know. Zephi has gone north already, and I'll leave with Deborah and Barak soon. Elam will stay behind with the men and wait for the signal to advance north He's already acting like their leader. You'd be proud of him as well. Pray for us. We'll return soon. Deborah said the battle wouldn't last long.

All my love,
Persis

I ran to catch up to the boy, but when he heard my footsteps, he whirled around with such speed that I jumped. We both stood quiet for a moment, staring at one another with wide eyes until I began to laugh.

"I'm sorry," I sputtered. "I didn't mean to startle you."

He had the largest brown eyes I've ever seen. They were sweet and sad at the same time. He offered a weak smile. "It's all right," he mumbled.

"I remember you," I told him.

He shifted from one foot to the other. "I remember you too."

"You're going home?"

"Yes," he admitted in a small voice. His shoulders were hunched, and he hung his head in a miserable way.

I knew he was running away because he was afraid, but I didn't despise him for it. I felt sorry for him. I reached out my hand and touched his arm. "It's all right," I reassured him. "Perhaps God needs you at home to help protect our town.

If every man went to war, who would be left to keep the peace in our homes?"

I held out my hand and showed him the paper folded inside it. "Would you give this to my mother and father when you return? I'd like them to know that my brother and I are safe."

He took the paper from me. "I'd be honored to deliver a message for Persis, armor bearer of Deborah," he announced with a sudden twinkle in his eyes.

My surprise must have been mirrored in my face, because he laughed this time. "Everyone knows," he said.

He turned on his heels and strode away, but not before I cried out to him, "Wait! I don't even know your name!"

"It's Amal," he called over his shoulder. As I walked away, I thought that I'd a found a new friend in this Amal.

Diary Three

Kedesh-naphtali and Mount Tabor

Under Cover of Night

My days and nights have been reversed. My day began at dusk and is ending now at dawn. I left with Deborah and Barak when the rest of the camp was finishing their supper and settling down for the evening. Deborah said it's best to travel under cover of night in case there are spies lurking in the hills. It was just as well. I was so nervous I wouldn't have slept anyway.

Now I'll be lucky if I can put my thoughts on paper before my eyelids drop. The sun will beat above us in a short while, but we're settled in a thick grove of shady trees and bushes near a tributary of the Jordan River.

I thought I'd be loaded down with arms, and I questioned my ability to carry such heavy equipment as we trudged through valleys and over hills for the whole of this night and the next two.

I was surprised when the two snowy white donkeys and one mottled one draped with scarlet saddle blankets were led into the camp.

Wooden saddles covered with leather sat on top of the blankets. The mottled donkey, which I knew was intended for my use, was loaded with water skins and bags of food to last the next few days. The extra arms were also strapped to the donkeys.

I was about to mount my donkey, when I heard a step behind me. My heart leapt when I saw Elam! I thought he'd come to see me off, but then I saw Deborah emerge from her tent and incline her head toward him. Elam met with her for several minutes. As it turns out, he was made the captain of the force that will wait at Ephraim! I'm so proud of him; I can't even speak of it without my eyes tearing.

Deborah carried one ruby-studded sword in a scabbard around her waist. She supplied me with my own scabbard and a bronze dagger. Elam carried three new shields. He said they were for Deborah, Barak, and me. I ran my hand over the familiar, supple skin. When I turned it over, I saw what I was looking for. The letter *M* was stitched above the seam.

Elam showed me how to hold Deborah's iron spear upright in my right hand while I guided the donkey with my left. I trotted around the camp for quite some time, weaving around the tents until I felt comfortable carrying the weapons and riding at the same time. The donkey was faster and stronger than any I had ridden before.

When it was time to leave, Elam pulled me down and whispered in my ear. "You're carrying your hide written in blood, aren't you?"

I told him I was, but he made me pull it from the pocket of my girdle and show it to him.

"It's probably silly, but I'll feel better if you keep it close to you," he told me. "I know that God is the only protection you need and he goes before you. He'll be with you, and he'll be with Deborah and Barak. Don't lose sight of that no matter what your eyes show you in the days ahead. God's glory will be revealed in time. Don't forget that."

"Will I see you soon?" I asked.

He nodded. "You'll see me. You'll also see Zephi and another whom you know. Now you must go."

I didn't have time to ask Elam what he meant. It was time to leave. We rode all night in the moonlight and didn't stop until the sun rose over the hills in the east.

More of the Story

When we stopped, Barak led the donkeys to drink and I made a fire. Deborah helped me bake bread on a stone heated in the flames. I felt better after we ate; the warmth of the food calmed my stomach. Unfortunately, it did nothing to alleviate my fears. Deborah noticed that I was troubled, and she asked me what was on my mind.

"Armor bearers are chosen for their loyalty and courage. Isn't that true?" I asked her.

"It's true," she replied.

"Deborah, I do pledge my loyalty to you and to God and to my country," I told her. "But I don't feel courageous right now. I'd be lying to you if I didn't admit that I'm afraid. Perhaps, if it isn't too late, there would be another better suited to serve you."

Barak had returned with the donkeys, and Deborah motioned for me to move away from the morning fire. We sat together on a soft bed of grass. Yellow and purple wildflowers sprouted in tiny bunches. I fingered the tiny petals while I waited for her to speak.

I watched her smooth her lilac robes around her. The slight wind stirred her long hair and blew a strand into her face. Here I was, sitting beside a prophetess, a judge, a military commander—the highest leader in the land—and yet she seemed so normal. She seemed like one of us. I could almost imagine my mother and father inviting her to supper!

"Persis," she began, "those who possess courage are afraid. They smell fear when the odor of death drifts to their nostrils. They taste fear when they inhale the bitterness of war, which laces the air. They see fear mirrored in the eyes of the wounded and dying. The difference is that they don't shirk from it. This is courage.

"We write history with every step we take closer to Mount Tabor. We all know that there are no guarantees. Israel will be victorious. God promised as much, but we don't know how many of us will live to tell the tale. Am I afraid? Of course. Is Barak afraid? Of course. Are you afraid? You should be. You carry weapons into battle for the first time. Will you march on despite your fears?"

"Yes," I told her.

"Then you possess courage."

We walked back toward our cozy camp, and Deborah put her arm around my shoulders. "You're a special girl, Persis," she told me. "It was clear from the first time I laid eyes on you that you possessed the qualities of a great servant and a born leader. You came to me in the night because your loyalty and courage compelled you. I'm glad you're here with me."

Every word Deborah speaks is filled with wisdom. Her work ethic is that of a soldier and laborer, yet this wisdom she possesses along with her strength and empathy elevates her to that of a great leader. I want to learn from her. God, make me a sponge so that I can absorb every drop of her wise teachings.

A Fright by the River—the Next Day

I must tell you what has happened. We stopped again just before daybreak. The sky to the east was a pale blue, but the sun hadn't yet risen. The morning was still dark and shadowy.

We made camp again by another tributary of the Jordan River, this one snaking to the east toward the mountains of Gilead. I offered to water the donkeys this time. My bottom was sore, and my legs were stiff from riding all day. I led the donkeys down a steep, brush-covered slope. The bend here was shallow and the bank was swampy, so I stood and waited. I watched the animals dip their muzzles into the cool water. My thoughts drifted away until I heard the snap of a twig on the other side of the stream.

I looked up but saw nothing. I remembered hearing somewhere that the banks of the Jordan River were home to many wild animals. I chided myself for not being more alert. I quickly scanned the tall brush, though it would be impossible to see an animal crouched in the grass.

Snap! It was there again! This time the donkeys lifted their heads and pricked their ears. I sensed there was something waiting on the other side, though I didn't think it was an animal. I climbed down the bank and slowly walked to the animals. I grabbed their reigns, two in one hand and one in the other, and pulled them up the slope.

I heard it again, closer to me this time, and I ran as fast as I could back to the camp. The donkeys loped beside me. My heart pounded and I gasped for breath. Barak saw my face and drew his sword. Deborah's hand moved to her scabbard. I pulled out my own dagger and waited.

We heard a slight rustle, and Deborah whispered, "It's no animal. Someone is lurking there."

Barak took a step forward and called out, "Show yourselves at once, or I'll come after you. I'll drive this sword into your heart before you can change your mind."

There was a rustle again and then a voice called out, "Wait! It's your servant Amal. I've come to deliver a message to you!"

It Really Is Amal!

He crawled from the brush and stood up, his hands in front of him. There were leaves in his hair and red scratches on his cheek. His eyes appeared large in his face like the last time I saw him, but this time they were filled with purpose and confidence. "I come alone," he announced.

Barak stood still and turned toward Deborah. She nodded. "Lower your weapon. It's all right. He is indeed my messenger. "What news have you carried with you all this way, Amal?"

I stood and stared at the boy I had spoken to just the other day! I couldn't find words. I thought he was deserting the camp, and he led me to believe that he was. All this time, he'd been Deborah's secret messenger.

He looked at me and then back to Deborah.

"It's all right, Amal," Deborah said. "I believe you've met Persis. Whatever message you have for me can be shared in the presence of my trusted armor bearer."

I still wonder how Deborah knew I had met Amal.

He nodded. "Mushi the tanner has asked me to deliver the following message." He pulled out a scrap of papyrus and read: "Senaah knows of your movements and has informed Heber the Kenite that you will be amassing forces at Mount Tabor. Heber is sure to inform Sisera. They will be ready and waiting for you and your troops when you arrive."

I'm still shocked at the message I heard. How did Mushi know that Amal was Deborah's messenger? How did he know that Senaah knew of our movements? Mushi seems to know a lot of unusual things for a tanner. Perhaps he makes it his business to know and help in whatever way he can. Maybe that's why he made the shields. He can't supply the whole army with new equipment, but maybe he tries to serve in whatever capacity he is needed.

I'd heard about Heber the Kenite in the camp at Ephraim. The Kenites are descendants of Hobab, the brother-in-law of Moses. They were friendly with the Israelites for a long time, but in recent years Heber separated himself. He aligned himself with the Canaanites.

Deborah smiled when she heard the message. "All is well," she said.

I was startled by her words. Why was it good that Sisera had been informed of our movements?

"You have a traitor among you?" Barak asked her.

"There are many traitors, Barak. You know this. The beauty and danger of traitors is that they'll sell out to either side and back again in the blink of an eye. This time it has worked to our advantage. Zephi informed me of Senaah's allegiance long ago. So he's leaked word to Heber, which is what I had hoped for. Senaah isn't the surprise, here—Heber is."

"How so?' Barak asked her.

"No one knows that Heber has realigned himself with us. Sisera will think he's received covert word of our plans. In fact, he's being fed our movements. It is he who has to fear a traitor in his camp. God has a surprise in store for him."

Before Amal left, he sat with me for a moment. "I'm sorry I couldn't tell you earlier, Persis. No one else in the camp knows who I am, and we have to be very careful now. It's almost impossible to know for sure who can be trusted. As you can see, war is a very tricky business."

"I understand," I told him.

"Your father and mother already knew of your well-being," he told me. "Mushi has ways of gleaning information! They're very proud of you, by the way."

I'm shocked at how different Amal appeared today. I felt sorry for him the first time I saw him with his slumped shoulders and sad eyes. Today his entire countenance had changed. Now I understand why. He disappeared into the brush the same way he came, but he left with the promise to meet us at Kedesh.

This has been a day of many surprises. Now I understand what Elam meant when he said I would see another whom I know. And I agree with Amal about one thing. It's getting harder and harder to know who to trust.

Dawn

We have arrived at Kedesh-naphtali. The sunrise greeted us as we climbed the top of the ridge and looked out at the Sea of Chinnereth a short distance away. The lake is shaped like a giant harp, and it sparkled silver with the new morning rays. I noticed that the Jordan River begins its meandering journey at the southern tip of this body of water.

I was grateful for the start of the day, and my heart lightened a little as I watched the sky fill with light. The night had been dark in many ways. There was only a crescent moon to light our way, so we had to travel with extra caution.

I was filled with trepidation anyway after Amal's surprise visit. I froze in fear each time a branch stirred or a lizard scurried beneath the brush. I couldn't help but think that if Amal could hide among the dense foliage, who else could be hiding and waiting for us?

Sisera has many spies younger and spryer than Senaah. Perhaps they had followed us when we left Mount Ephraim. Had they waited to ambush us in the night? The evening had been blacker and more shadowy than the previous two. It would have been the perfect time to spring upon three weary travelers, and it wouldn't have mattered that two were military commanders and one was an armor bearer.

Barak had rested his hand on the handle of his sword several times, and I noticed Deborah doing the same. Barak has been uneasy since we left last night. Deborah noticed this too. I watched her look at him frequently with long, sideways glances.

All night I kept my spear upright, and my arm ached and my muscles twitched in exhaustion. I couldn't stop my thoughts, and I rode the entire way stiff and paralyzed with fear.

Then as we began our ascent up the sloping ridge, we passed a field of whitewashed tombs tucked into a hollow of the hill. Tombs are whitened to remind the Jews to stay clear of them. We moved as far away from them as we could. If we rode too close, we'd defile ourselves and become ceremonially unclean.

Zephi Brings Disturbing News—Noon

My joy at the sight of Zephi's kind, familiar face faded with the news he carried. Nine hundred of Sisera's war chariots were already amassed at the base of Mount Tabor. Mushi was right.

Senaah had told Heber of our movements, and Heber had passed the word to Sisera. Within an hour, Zephi said, the troops had left their base camp at Harosheth Haggoyim near Mount Carmel and moved southeast to Tabor.

Barak rode off on his white donkey. "I will return within two days with the force we need," he said.

The hill of Kedesh is cloaked with oak and terebinth trees. A short while ago, I sat with Zephi in the shade of a large bough. "It doesn't look good," he admitted. "Their war chariots are deadly. They have scythes, long curving blades, fastened to their wheels. When those chariots are driven into a band of our footmen, they'll be executed in a horrifying manner."

I shuddered at the picture he painted in my mind.

"I also saw heavily armed pikemen," he continued. "Do you know how they fight, Persis?"

I shook my head. I wasn't sure I wanted to know, but Zephi was intent on telling me.

"They group themselves together in rows. Each holds a shield and a pike. The pike is a wooden shaft twice the length of you with a pointed steel head. They move forward as one body and mow down their enemy. Our soldiers have no chance against them either. By the time they're close enough to use their short weapons, they'll be dead."

My stomach was queasy, and my head was light. I hadn't eaten for many hours, and I'd slept little. This news wasn't helping my spirits. "Zephi, don't you believe that God called Deborah to lead us to war?"

"I do," he said. "But I want you to know that his hand alone will deliver us. If we stare into the eyes of our enemy and gaze at the weapons of his warfare, our souls will sink before we begin to fight. Remember when you are by Deborah's side, looking toward the battleground spread before you—our champion has gone before us, and we will fight our war on his terms."

I'll bury those words deep in my heart. In the midst of the dark days I fear will come, I pray I can recall them and draw upon their hope and comfort.

Dusk

Amal just arrived, and Zephi greeted him with great joy. I suppose it should come as no surprise to me that they're friends! Amal was here just long enough to get off his donkey and stretch his legs when Deborah ordered him to deliver an urgent message.

"Ride to the hill of Moreh," she told him. "You will find our sentinel stationed at the observation post. Deliver this message: 'It is time. Our men at Ephraim must begin their advance north at once. Make haste.'"

Amal disappeared down the ridge. I heard the clomping of his donkey's hooves fade into the night. It wouldn't take him long to ride the short distance to Moreh. He'd deliver the message, and the sentinel would light a signal fire.

The sentry at the observation post on Mount Gilboa would be watching for it. Once he saw the flames, he'd light another signal fire. Elam, the captain of Ephraim's force, would lead his troops forward. In just a few hours, they'd be on their way.

Zephi left just after Amal. He would ride first to Mount Gilboa and then to the hill of Moreh to track our forces from Ephraim.

I stood with Deborah at the top of the ridge near our camp, and we gazed at the lake in the distance. The sky wasn't as clear as it had been in recent days. The stars were shrouded in a cloudy film, and the air felt thicker than usual. A puff of wind carried the fresh scent of rain from the hills beyond. I was troubled, and I decided to talk to Deborah about it.

"I know we'll march toward Mount Tabor when Barak returns with the men, but there is one thing I'm confused about," I told her. "If Elam and his force advance north and move toward Sisera on the open plain, how will they stand a chance against the Canaanites and their chariots? Have they been sent to their deaths?"

My heart pounded like a drum, and I thought for sure she could hear it. I was bold, perhaps too bold, to question our military commander on her tactical plans, but I felt Deborah was also my friend.

She smiled, and I let out the breath I held in my chest. She was kind and patient with her answer. It's what I've come to expect of Deborah. "Persis, now you will see the glory of God for perhaps the first time in your life. Once you witness his awesome power and might, you will be changed forever. This is all I can tell you."

Early the Next Day

The regiment of soldiers from the tribe of Naphtali has arrived. They marched up the ridge in perfect formation, carrying their standard high. They reminded me of a battalion of soldier ants. The cloth of their flag clung to a long wooden pole and waved its colors in the wind. On the front was a picture of a serpent.

It's impossible to count the men, but I know they number in the thousands. They've been oiling their bucklers and polishing their weapons in preparation for battle. I've heard it said that the tribe of Naphtali is known for their courage. The men are robust, and their spirits are strong and tough and independent. If this is the case, they should serve Deborah and Barak well in the coming days.

It's true that our weapons are no match for those of the Canaanites. From what I can see so far, our footmen are archers, swordsmen, and slingers. Our weapons are bows and arrows, sickle swords, doubled-edged swords, daggers, slings, and an occasional spear. Some of these are rusty.

Though we may not be armed with superior weapons, the skill of these men is something to behold. I watched an archer pull back his bow. His arrow soared for a distance of about two hundred paces. A tiny blade of grass thinner than the width of my smallest fingernail was split in two.

Then I watched a slinger pick up a long strip of woven wool. It was at least three cubits in length, with a wide pocket in the middle to hold the stone. Deborah said it's so long because it's used to hurl stones a great distance.

He secured one end to the fingers of his throwing hand. He held the other end between his thumb and forefinger. With one under-handed wind up, he hurled the smooth stone missile at least 440 paces! There's a rumor that these slingers can heave their stones at a hair and not miss!

Slingers are important because they can inflict great damage. Even if their stones are met with the armor of the enemy, they can still cause serious internal injury. No soldier, not even a charioteer, wants to be hit with a stone that flies through the air faster than a horse gallops across the plain.

Another Day Passes

Barak has returned! He was followed by a huge regiment of troops from the tribe of Zebulun and a small contingent from the tribes of Manasseh and Issachar. The leader of Zebulun carried their banner, a beautiful one of three colors—silver, golden brown, and blood red—which bore the figure of a lion's cub. Issachar marched beneath the same flag, and Manasseh waved a banner that bore the figure of a boy.

There are so many men I can't believe it. We may not outnumber the Canaanites, but it's the largest group of soldiers I've ever seen gathered in one place. Deborah requested at least ten thousand men, but Barak thinks the number is closer to twenty thousand! I can believe it.

The men have no armor but their shields to protect them. Zephi told me the other day that the Canaanites are protected by bronze scale armor. Sometimes they wear mail coats made of metal scales stitched right to the garment. This thought sobers me. It's another reminder that we must rely on God alone for our protection. Without him we're defenseless against such a well-equipped and powerful foe.

Sunup

A quick word until later. We'll move out within the hour. All of our troops have arrived, so there's no reason to prolong the inevitable. We'll march toward Mount Tabor and look upon our enemy with our own eyes for the very first time. My heart pumps with energy and anticipation. I have no time to fear. That will come later.

Evening at Mount Tabor

We've just arrived. Though we didn't have to travel far, it took us longer than I expected. There are so many of us now that it takes quite some time for us to cover a short distance. Can you imagine the sight of twenty thousand troops snaking up the mountain? I'm humbled when I think of Moses leading two million of our people out of Egypt. It's in times like this, God, when I feel so small and you seem so big.

Mount Tabor stands by itself in the Plain of Esdraelon. In the light of day, I'll be able to see the Great Sea to the northwest as well as the plains spread out below. We're camped in the oval plain area on the top.

It's a spooky feeling to know that our enemies are camped beneath us. We're quiet and so are they. Our sentries are posted around the perimeter of our camp, which is very large. I can see their shadows walk back and forth, their swords poised in their hands. Every now and then the metal of the blade glints in the firelight.

It's not likely that there will be a surprise attack. Sisera needs us to move off the mountain into the valley below so he can make use of his chariots. Still, it's a comfort to know that there are guards all around me.

Deborah and Barak are conferring beside the light of a small lamp. The morning will come sooner than I want. I'll sleep now.

Midmorning

It's a quiet day. There's no sign of movement from either camp. Sisera lies in wait beneath us. His forces have already circled the base of the mountain. Barak paces back and forth. Even the men are growing restless. Deborah says it isn't time to move yet.

The filmy clouds that I noticed days ago on the ridge of Kadesh have moved southwest with us. Now they're thick and heavy, and the sky is the color of a dirty blade. I know we can't lie in wait like this for very long. There's too much tension.

One Day Passes

There's trouble! Amal rode into camp in the shadow of sunrise, white and shaken. Our troops at Ephraim have met resistance from the kings of Canaan in the Valley of Jezreel. The townspeople sprang upon our men in a surprise attack in Taanach by the waters of Megiddo late yesterday. When Amal left, the fierce fighting had ended, but some of our men were killed by the sword, and some of theirs died as well. Elam, he said, was fine and out of the line of danger. Thank you, Lord!

"It looks like our victory is assured and the Canaanites are retreating," Amal said. "Zephi asked me to send this message: 'Our force from Ephraim will arrive in the lowlands by the River Kishon this afternoon. Expect Sisera to divert his forces from Tabor to assist his allies in the attack against our men.'"

Deborah nodded and turned her head toward the sky. It was an hour past sunrise, but the sky was dark and ominous. A light wind blew her hair across her face. A black scarf skipped across the camp and disappeared into the trees.

"Warn the troops that we will descend the mountain in one hour. Tell them that the Lord God goes before us," Deborah told Barak. "By then, Sisera will have moved his men south, away from the base of Tabor. By the time we descend the mountain and he discovers our presence close at hand, we will see the Lord within our midst."

I must get ready now. The time has come. I will carry Deborah's shield and her extra weapons—her spear, a dagger, and a double-edged sword. I've touched the hide inside my girdle. It's still there.

I feel a cold ball in the pit of my stomach. The air is warm and heavy, but my skin is clammy. My feet feel like bricks mortared to the dirt.

My thoughts drift toward Mama and Papa. I'm sure it's because my memories of them give me peace and comfort. What is it also that Elam told me? "No matter what your eyes show you in the days ahead . . . God's glory will be revealed in time."

Diary Four

The Kishon River, Mount Tabor, and

Bethel

Into Battle

The battle that I will record now has been over for several hours. I couldn't tell you about it before this moment. I'll try to put down the events in as much detail as I can remember. So much happened . . .

Barak stood on a large rock in the middle of the camp, and all of the regiments looked toward him. Deborah was on my right. Amal was near Zephi, who had just arrived. A drop of rain fell on my arm, and I looked up. The sky wasn't gray anymore; it was dark like dusk. The wind had died, and the air was still. Not a leaf stirred.

"Men!" Barak cried. "The time has come to gather your weapons and fight." His voice was strong and unwavering. "Physically we are no match against the prowess of our enemy, but spiritually our enemy is no match against the prowess of our Lord! We must furnish ourselves with courage! God has gone before us to prepare our way and to defeat the enemy. His presence is at hand. Do not fear!"

The men raised their voices together and held up their weapons. They organized themselves into two attacking divisions; the one in the rear served as the reserve. If Barak needed to escape, the rear troops would act as his defense. Spearmen formed the front line, followed by the archers and then the slingers.

The entire force stood behind Barak, who was poised at the edge of the mountain. They were ready to charge the moment Barak held up his sword. Suddenly, I saw him scan the horizon. His eyes were filled with fear, and his stature seemed shrunken. Deborah saw it too, and she hastened toward him. She stood behind him to shield his appearance from the soldiers.

"Barak," she whispered with urgency. "Now when they seem most threatening is the time they are ripe for ruin. This thing is already done."

Barak gazed at her, and I watched the cloud lift from his eyes. A light filled his face, and he nodded with sudden understanding. Then an amazing thing happened. He raised his sword high into the air so all who were behind him might see it. At that instant a bolt of white lightning pierced the dark sky and lit up his silver sword as if it were on fire.

"Go!" Deborah shouted. "This is the day the LORD has given Sisera into your hands! Has not the LORD gone ahead of you?"

Barak charged down the mountain with his sword thrust forward. Thousands of men raced after him, their weapons lifted in their arms as they flew. Deborah, Zephi, Amal, and I watched the battle unfold below us.

Sisera's chariots were so numerous I couldn't count them. They crouched like black leopards, ready to spring upon their prey in the wide, open valley. The bronze helmets of the horsemen sparked with fire, and their iron swords flashed.

Our force from Ephraim was charging from the rear. They bounded through the valley toward the Kishon River. Barak and his force had divided in two, attacking the flanks of Sisera and his men.

The Canaanites had been caught off guard. They faced all directions now. Their pikemen grouped together as Zephi had said they would, uniting their shields like one large shell. The long pikes pointed up, forward, and sideways. The bowmen loaded their arrows and drew back their strings. The javelin throwers held their arms above their heads, their long weapons poised, ready for flight.

My fingers dug into my arms as I watched Sisera's horsemen lift up their whips. They snapped their leather straps down upon their horses with such force that the sharp cracks echoed through the valley over and over again. The horses reared up, their front hooves pawing wildly at the air.

Then, as they dug in their heels and began their charge toward our men, the sky split open and a thunderous roar shook the earth. Rain and hailstones the size of slingers' stones poured from the black clouds. They pummeled the faces of Sisera's men with such ferocity that they had no choice but to hold their shields above their heads. The dry riverbed filled with water almost at once. The black soil soaked up the water and softened and turned into a thick mud. It groped at the ankles of Sisera's men and horses and clutched at the wheels of the chariots.

Lightning shot from the clouds in every direction and sent the horses into a frightened frenzy. They kicked up their hooves and tried to pull themselves and their chariot wheels out of the murk, which grew deeper and deeper with the falling rain.

Finally Barak saw that it was time. He raised his sword once again, and his men descended upon the Canaanites like a cloud of bees. The force from Ephraim did the same, and I saw Elam charge into the midst of the enemy soldiers.

I heard the clash of metal against metal and the scream of the horses as they slid beneath the swirling river. I covered my ears when the slingers shots hit their marks and the men screamed in agony.

Hour after hour we watched as the Canaaites were struck down. When it was apparent that they couldn't win, they retreated. They ran on foot in every direction, but Barak and our soldiers were on their heels.

Deborah turned suddenly and reached for Zephi's hand. "The coward Sisera has jumped off his chariot and deserted his men. He's escaped on foot. I saw him run east. Follow him and don't let him out of your sight. Amal, go with him. Report to me on his whereabouts."

One by one our soldiers trudged up the mountain. I glanced one last time at the valley below me. It was a red sea of carnage. The limp bodies of soldiers and horses littered the mud. Their iron weapons had fallen like toys beside them.

After the Battle

I hadn't seen Elam return, but there was no time to think. Many of the men were hurt and needed care. Deborah and I tore up strips of cloth and tied them above the soldiers' gaping wounds to stop the bleeding. We tore larger strips with three sides to make slings so their arms could rest against their bodies.

Word of our victory trickled out. In a few hours men and women from the surrounding villages climbed the mountain. The men pulled carts so the wounded could return home. The women brought food, and they dished up hot stews and bread for the soldiers. One of them even pulled me aside and wrapped me in a thick wool blanket. I hadn't realized that I was soaked to the bone and shaking.

I heard a familiar voice beside me and turned to see Elam! He was battered and bleeding from several cuts on his head. His hair was matted to his skin with dried, crusty blood, but he was smiling! I wrapped my arms around him and hugged him as I tight as I dared.

Then I began to cry. I was filled with pent-up emotion. We were safe, and God had protected us! Deborah was right. I'd seen and felt the glory of God for the very first time. It was unlike anything I'd ever experienced in my life. It had changed me in a moment, and I knew then that I'd never be the same.

The Next Day

Many of our soldiers have returned. They said they followed Barak in pursuit of the Canaanites as far as Harosheth Haggoyim. Not a single one of our enemies was left standing.

"Where is Barak now?" Deborah asked one of them.

"He went in pursuit of Sisera," they told her.

We're still waiting for Zephi and Amal to return with news of Sisera's whereabouts. Perhaps they'll meet Barak on the way. Deborah can't proclaim victory until his presence is accounted for.

A New Day-Early Morning

At last! Our three missing have returned. General Barak, Zephi, and Amal rode into camp together. Zephi said he and Amal followed Sisera past our original camp at Kadesh northward toward Hazor. The boundary of Naphtali was known as "the oakwood at the twin tents of wandering." This was where Heber the Kenite had pitched his tent. This is where Sisera had hoped to find safety and refuge.

"When did you meet up with Barak?" Deborah asked.

"Much later," Zephi explained. "Jael, Heber's wife, was waiting at the tent door when Sisera arrived. We think she was awaiting news from the army or the outcome of the battle. When she saw Sisera, she went out to meet him. 'Come, my lord, come right in,' she told him. 'Don't be afraid.'

"Sisera was in a bad state," Zephi continued. "Shaken, bloodied, and exhausted. We crept closer to the tent and could see their shadows and hear their hushed voices. She put a covering over him, and we heard him say, 'I'm thirsty. Please give me some water.'

"Jael opened a skin of milk instead and helped him sit up so he could drink it. She covered him back up then."

"We think Sisera was nervous," Amal added. "He told her repeatedly, 'Stand in the doorway of the tent. If someone comes by and asks you, 'Is anyone here?' say 'No.'

"It was silent for a long time," Amal continued. "Jael went to the door several times and looked out. We hid ourselves each time. After a while we heard faint snores, and we knew Sisera had fallen into a deep sleep."

Zephi and Amal were quiet for a moment.

"Come," Deborah implored, "don't leave me in suspense. What happened next. Where is Sisera now?"

"He's dead," Zephi stated. "By the hand of Jael. We heard a scuffle and a commotion and then silence again. That's when Barak arrived. Jael heard him and went outside. 'Come,' she told him. 'I will show you the man you're looking for.' When Barak entered the tent, he found

Sisera dead. A tent peg had been hammered through his temple."

I listened to Zephi, and I felt my heart soar. I remembered Deborah's words to Barak in the Valley of Ephraim not long after he arrived on his white donkey. "Very well," she'd told him when asked to accompany him into battle. "I will go with you. But because of the way you are going about this, the honor will not be yours, for the LORD will hand Sisera over to a woman."

The woman Deborah had spoken of was Jael! So many moons have come and gone since I left Bethel. I think I've lived a hundred years in less than one! I've seen so much with my eyes. I've felt so much in my heart. I've learned so much about God's might, power, and majesty as well as his love, tenderness, and protection.

Deborah was an ordinary woman once, but God made her great because she was content to serve him first in ordinary ways. Now she'll be remembered always as an extraordinary leader! And I—ordinary Persis—was privileged enough to serve beside her.

A Celebration of Song

It's our final day at Mount Tabor. Tomorrow we'll return to our homes. It's been the most glorious day. The men and women of the villages have continued to bring food to our camp. Tonight we had a victory feast. Fishermen brought their catches from the Sea of Chinnereth. There were baskets of sardines, blenny, barbel, and silurus, which we roasted over the fire.

We ate parched corn from the lush fields in the valley. From the banks of the Jordan River came bananas, oranges, dates, mangoes, lemons, almonds, and peaches! I haven't eaten this well in a very long time. Even at my home at Bethel, our food supplies were always scant and our meals were filling but bland.

Elam says that will all change now. The Canaanites have been subdued, and prosperity will return to our land again. He said it's important, though, that our people never turn their backs on God again. We must keep him in the center of our lives.

Deborah wrote a beautiful song of victory, and she and Barak sang it together. The villagers brought their instruments. There was a lyre and a lute, sistrums, tambourines, and pipes. It was a reminder to all of us that God is our faithful deliverer. Deborah has allowed me to copy down her song in the back pages of my diary, but I wanted to share my favorite part with you now:

"From the heavens the stars fought,
   from their courses they fought
against Sisera.
The river Kishon swept them away,
   the age-old river, the river Kishon.
   March on, my soul; be strong!"

I never will forget what happened on the day God scattered our enemies. I hope that through Deborah's song and through the pages of my diary, my children and grandchildren will be able to relive the day God's glory was revealed—the day the stars fought from the heavens.

The Song of Deborah

"When the princes in Israel take the lead,
　　when the people willingly offer themselves—
　　praise the LORD!

"Hear this, you kings! Listen, you rulers!
　　I will sing to the LORD, I will sing;
　　I will make music to the LORD, the God
　　of Israel.

"O LORD, when you went out from Seir,
　　when you marched from the land of Edom,
the earth shook, the heavens poured,
　　the clouds poured down water.
The mountains quaked before the LORD, the One
　　of Sinai,
　　before the LORD, the God of Israel.

"In the days of Shamgar son of Anath,
　　in the days of Jael, the roads were abadoned;
　　travelers took to winding paths.
Village life in Israel ceased,
　　ceased until I, Deborah, arose,
　　arose a mother in Israel.

When they chose new gods,
　　war came to the city gates,
and not a shield or spear was seen
　　among forty thousand in Israel.
My heart is with Israel's princes,
　　with the willing volunteers among the people.
　　Praise the LORD!

"You who ride on white donkeys,
　　sitting on your saddle blankets,
　　and you who walk along the road,
consider the voice of the singers at the
　　watering places.
　　They recite the righteous acts of the LORD,
　　the righteous acts of his warriors in Israel.

"Then the people of the LORD
　　went down to the city gates.
'Wake up, wake up, Deborah!
　　Wake up, wake up, break out in song!
Arise, O Barak!
　　Take captive your captives, O son of Abinoam.'

"Then the men who were left
　　came down to the nobles;
the people of the LORD

came to me with the mighty.
Some came from Ephraim, whose roots were in Amalek;
    Benjamin was with the people who followed you.
From Makir captains came down,
    from Zebulun those who bear a commander's staff.
The princes of Issachar were with Deborah;
    yes, Issachar was with Barak,
    rushing after him into the valley.
In the districts of Reuben
    there was much searching of heart.
Why did you stay among the campfires
    to hear the whistling for the flocks?
In the districts of Reuben
    there was much searching of heart.
Gilead stayed beyond the Jordan.
    And Dan, why did he linger by the ships?
Asher remained on the coast and stayed in his coves.
The people of Zebulun risked their very lives;
    so did Naphtali on the heights of the field.

"Kings came, they fought;
    the kings of Canaan fought
at Taanach by the waters of Megiddo,
    but they carried off no silver, no plunder.
From the heavens the stars fought,
    from their courses they fought against Sisera.

The river Kishon swept them away,
> the age-old river, the river Kishon.
> March on, my soul; be strong!
Then thundered the horses' hoofs—
> galloping, galloping go his mighty steeds.
'Curse Meroz,' said the angel of the LORD.
> 'Curse its people bitterly,
because they did not come to help the Lord,
> to help the LORD against the mighty.'

"Most blessed of women be Jael,
> the wife of Heber the Kenite,
> most blessed of tent-dwelling women.
He asked for water, and she gave him milk;
> in a bowl fit for nobles she brought him curdled milk.
Her hand reached for the tent peg,
> her right hand for the workman's hammer.
She struck Sisera, she crushed his head,
> she shattered and pierced his temple.
At her feet he sank,
> he fell; there he lay,
At her feet he sank, he fell;
> where he sank, there he fell—dead.
"Through the window peered Sisera's mother;
> behind the lattice she cried out,
'Why is his chariot so long in coming?

Why is the clatter of his chariots delayed?'
The wisest of her ladies answer her;
    indeed, she keeps saying to herself,
'Are they not finding and dividing the spoils:
    a girl or two for each man,
    colorful garments as plunder for Sisera,
    colorful garments embroidered,
    highly embroidered garments for my neck—
all this as plunder?'

"So may all your enemies perish, O LORD!
    But may they who love you be like the sun
    when it rises in its strength."

Epilogue

Following the defeat of the Canaanites, Deborah ruled for forty years beneath the Palm of Deborah in the Valley of Ephraim. During this time the Israelites had peace from all of their oppressors.

Though the details of Deborah's life after the great battle with Sisera are not known, it is believed that she died at the end of her recorded rule in the year 1169 B.C. What became of Barak after he and Deborah celebrated their victory remains a mystery.

Senaah the traitor was never heard from again. When word of the Israelites' victory spread to Bethel, a group of townspeople, including Mushi the tanner and Obadiah, surrounded his small stone house. They demanded entrance but heard only the echoes of their own voices.

They broke down the door only to find an empty house. Senaah had fled, probably in the early hours of the morning when he realized the Canaanites' defeat was imminent. In his haste he left behind proof of his alliance with Sisera, including detailed notes of his conversations with the general and maps of the Canaanite headquarters at Harosheth Haggoyim.

Mushi was over 140 years old when he died. After his death Zephi revealed that the wise and kindly tanner had been a spy for Ehud, the judge who had served prior to Deborah. It was through Mushi's efforts that Ehud was able to penetrate the palace of King Eglon and escape undetected.

Mushi had recruited and trained Zephi at an early age. As Persis and others discovered later, Mushi had also made all of the shields, girdles, and slings for the upper echelons of the Israelite army.

Amal continued to serve as a courier for Deborah, delivering messages throughout the land of Israel for the next forty years.

During the four decades of peace that followed the battle with Sisera, Zephi's services as a spy were no longer needed. He returned to Bethel, where he lived a peaceful and sedentary life raising flocks. Persis visited him often. She, Amal, and Zephi remained friends for the rest of their lives.

Elam rose to great prominence after commanding the forces at Ephraim. He was promoted to a member of the Guard and served Deborah faithfully for a number of years. Eventually, he married a girl name Elisabeth, and they had four children. They settled in Bethel near his mother and father, and he practiced the trade of tent making until his death at a very old age.

Persis also married, much to her parents' delight, and bore two girls. Prior to her marriage, she was tutored by Deborah's scribe and eventually served as the first female clerk in ancient history. She organized public records, prepared drafts of wills, and brought all complaints or requests from the people to Deborah.

Twenty years after Deborah's death and five years after the passing of Persis's husband,

Persis's daughters went to her small stone house to check on her. They discovered that she had died peacefully in her sleep during the night. Her diaries, neatly rolled and tied with string, were on the bed beside her. On the other side of her was a ruby-crusted sword and an iron spear.

A copy of her will, penned in her own hand, was left beside her mattress. In it she allocated all of her possessions, however few, to her two girls. She also made one request: "Please find a way to tell the story of this battle. Let the world know how the glory of the Lord was revealed on this day."

The girls vowed that they would.

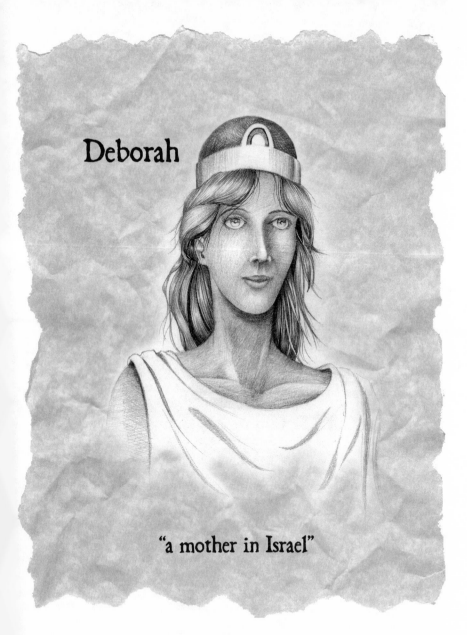

Deborah

"a mother in Israel"

Barak,
military leader of the Israelites

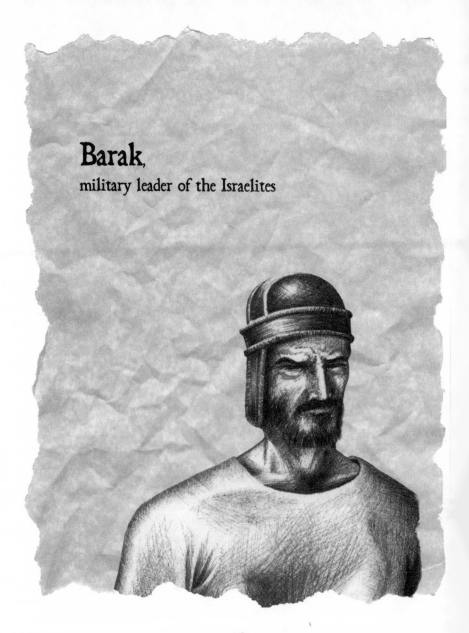

Deborah held court beneath a tall palm tree in the Valley of Ephraim. It was called the "palm of Deborah."

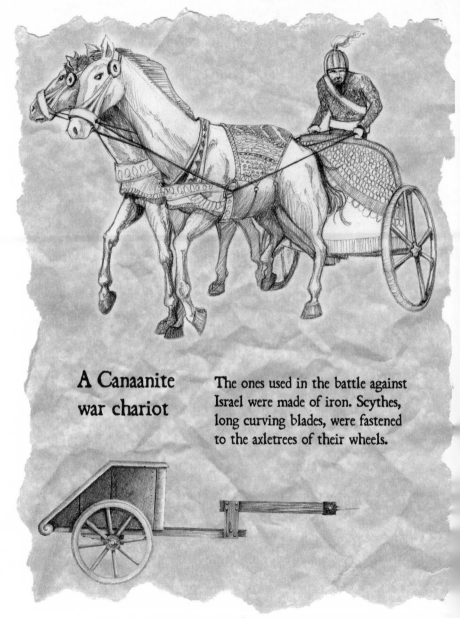

A Canaanite war chariot

The ones used in the battle against Israel were made of iron. Scythes, long curving blades, were fastened to the axletrees of their wheels.

The slingshot was made of a long strip of woven wool or leather with a wide pocket in the middle to hold the stone.

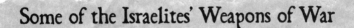

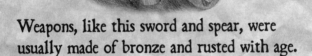

Weapons, like this sword and spear, were usually made of bronze and rusted with age.

Military leaders set up tents at their headquarters to discuss strategy.

Ancient tents were often made of goat hair. Ropes were attached to toggles, sewn into the tent, then tied to stakes, like this one, which were driven into the ground.

Deborah's Victory over Sisera

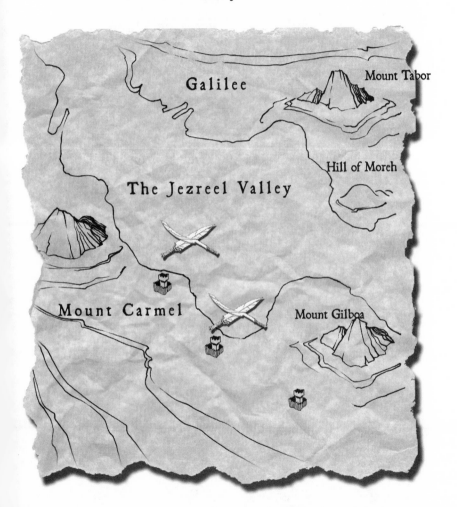

Persis's Home

The story takes place in the town of Bethel in Israel. It moves to the Valley of Ephraim, to Kedesh-naphtali, to Mount Tabor, and to the Valley of Jezreel. It is set (approximately) in the year 1200 B.C.

The People Persis Wrote of Most:

Deborah: Israel's fourth judge, prophetess, and military leader

Barak: Commander of the Israelite forces

Herself: Deborah's armor bearer *

Sisera: Commander of the Canaanite forces

Elam: Persis's older brother, commander of Israel's force at Ephraim*

Mushi: Town tanner and family friend *

Zephi: Spy for Israel and friend to Persis and Elam *

Amal: Courier to Deborah *

Senaah: Jewish traitor and spy for Sisera *

Mama: Persis's mother *

Papa: Persis's father *

The People Persis Encountered:
(in order of appearance)

Tabeal: Town baker *
Chuza: Town potter *
Scribe: Deborah's record keeper and a
doctor of law *
Heber the Kenite: Husband of Jael
Regiment of Naphtali: Large number of
soldiers from Israel's tribe of Naphtali
Regiment of Zebulun: Large number of
soldiers from Israel's tribe of Zebulun
Contingent of Manasseh: Small group of
soldiers from Israel's tribe of Manasseh
Contingent of Issachar: Small group of
soldiers from Israel's tribe of Issachar
Jael: Wife of Heber the Kenite, Sisera's
murderer

* denotes fictional characters

Tracing History:
A Timeline of Israel's Judges

1446 B.C.
Moses leads the Israelites out of Egypt.

1406 B.C.
Joshua leads the Israelites out of the wilderness into Canaan.

1375 B.C.
The period of the judges begins.

1367–1327 B.C.—Othniel
He is the first of the seven judges to deliver Israel from foreign oppression. Under his leadership, Israel is freed from the bondage of King Cushan-Rishathaim and the Arameans. Forty years of peace follows.

1309–1229 B.C.—Ehud
The left-handed judge kills King Eglon and leads Israel to victory over the Moabites. Israel has peace for eighty years until Ehud's death.

Sometime between 1229 B.C. and 1209 B.C.—Shamgar

He kills six hundred Philistines using only an ox goad as his weapon. He is said to have prepared the way for Deborah to fully deliver Israel from Canaanite oppression.

1209–1169 B.C.—Deborah

The Canaanites oppress Israel for twenty years following Ehud's death. Under Deborah's leadership, Israel defeats Sisera and the Canaanites. Peace ensues for forty years.

1162–1122 B.C.—Gideon

Through Gideon's faithful leadership, 300 Israelites defeat an army of 135,000 Midianites. He serves as judge in Israel for forty years.

Sometime between 1122 B.C. and 1075 B.C.—Jephthah

He soundly defeats the Ammonites, who have oppressed Israel for many years. He judges for six years.

1075–1055 B.C.—Samson

He is most famous for his supernatural strength. He has countless victories over the Philistines and rules Israel for twenty years.

1055–1050 B.C.—Samuel

He is a prophet, a priest, and the last judge of Israel. The Israelites tell Samuel that they want to be ruled by a king. Samuel anoints Saul, and he becomes Israel's first king.

1050 B.C.

Saul is anointed king.

*Lesser known judges include Tola, Jair, Ibzan, Elon, and Abdon

The Judges' Place in History

When Moses led the Israelites out of Egypt, he divided them into groups. A judge was appointed to each unit to oversee the affairs of the people and settle their arguments. Only the most important cases were brought before Moses.

A similar system was used after Joshua led the Israelites into Canaan. The land was divided into twelve areas that represented the twelve tribes of Israel. A judge ruled over one tribe or a group of tribes. These judges were the principal leaders in Israel from the time of Joshua's death to the reign of Saul, Israel's first king. Their roles were wide and varied.

They were the highest leaders of the land, the military commanders, and the administrators of justice. They were religious leaders because they acted as God's spokesmen, and they were known as saviors because they delivered the Israelites from their enemies.

Judges were not paid, they held the office for life, and they could not appoint their successors. In addition, the title could not be passed on to their children.

As administrators of justice, the judges held court in the city square, and the people would bring their cases to them. Exceptions include Samuel, who traveled from city to city to hold court, and Deborah, who held court beneath the palm tree in the Valley of Ephraim. It was known throughout the land as the "Palm of Deborah."

Then and Now

Bethel, first known as Luz, was mentioned seventy-two times in the Old Testament. It was located twelve miles north of Jerusalem, west of Ai, on the border of Ephraim.

Founded in about 2000 B.C., Bethel occupied an important place in history for both geographical and religious reasons. It lay on Israel's main north-south road and also at the junction of an east-west road, which connected it to the coastal plains.

The inhabitants of Bethel were fortunate: They had an abundance of springs on the city's high ridge and never had to rely on cisterns for water storage. Their land was fertile and excellent for raising a variety of crops.

When Abraham entered Canaan, he pitched his tent on the "mountain east of Bethel." He built an altar to the Lord there and called upon his name. He sojourned to Egypt, but when he returned he set up his tent between Bethel and Ai.

Some time later his grandson Jacob spent a night in Bethel and dreamed of a ladder that climbed into heaven. When he awoke, he exclaimed:

> "Surely the LORD is in this place, and I was not aware of it." He was afraid and said, "How awesome is this place! This is none other than the house of God; this is the gate of heaven."
>
> Genesis 28:18–19

From that time on, Luz was referred to as Bethel, which means "house of God."

After the Israelites entered the Promised Land, they carried the Ark of the Covenant to Bethel, where it was kept under the watchful eye of the high priest Phinehas, Aaron's grandson. During times of trouble, the Israelites journeyed here to seek God's counsel.

Today the ruins of the ancient city of Bethel lie near the modern city of Beitin in Israel. A Byzantine monastery dating to the fifth or sixth century A.D. commemorates the story of Jacob's dream in which he envisioned a ladder that reached into the heavens.

A ruined watchtower sits on the spot where Abraham is believed to have pitched his tent.

Bibliography

Many sources were consulted and used in research for writing Persis's and Deborah's story in the Promised Land Diaries series, including:

Adam Clarke's Commentary on the Bible, Adam Clarke, abridged by Ralph H. Earle (World Bible Publishing Co., 1996).

Atlas of the Bible: An Illustrated Guide to the Holy Land, edited by Joseph L. Gardner (The Readers Digest Association, 1981).

Battles of the Bible, Chaim Herzog and Mordechai Gichon (Greenhill Books, 1997).

The Biblical Times, edited by Derek Williams (Baker Books, a division of Baker Book House Company, 1997).

Fighting Techniques of the Ancient World, 3000 BC–AD 500: Equipment, Combat Skills, and Tactics, Simon Anglim, Phyllis G. Jestice, Rob S. Rice, Scott M. Rusch, John Serrati (Amber Books, 2002)

Jamieson, Fausset, and Brown's Commentary on the Whole Bible, Fausset, Brown, Robert Jamieson (Zondervan, 1999).

Matthew Henry's Commentary on the Whole Bible: Complete and Unabridged in One Volume, Matthew Henry (Hendrickson Publishers, 1991).

Meredith's Book of Bible Lists, J. L. Meredith (Bethany House Publishers, 1980).

Nelson's Illustrated Encyclopedia of the Bible, edited by John Drane (Thomas Nelson, Inc., 2001).

The New International Dictionary of the Bible, revising editor J. D. Douglas, general editor Merrill C. Tenney (Zondervan 1987).

The Picture Bible Dictionary, Berkeley and Alvera Mickelsen (Chariot Books, an imprint of David C. Cook Publishing Co., 1993).

Women of the Bible: A One-Year Devotional Study of Women in Scripture, Ann Spangler and Jean Syswerda (Zondervan, 1999).

Warriors of the Old Testament, Mark Healy (Firebird Books, 1989).

About the Author

Anne Tyra Adams is the author of eight children's books, several of which have been translated into three foreign languages: Indonesian, Korean, and Afrikaans. Two of her books, *The New Kids Book of Bible Facts* and *The Baker Book of Bible Travels for Kids,* provided the foundation for writing this series, the Promised Land Diaries.

A journalist and detailed researcher, Adams is also a "student of ancient history," with a deep fascination for the Jewish culture. She used all this experience, love of history, and curiosity to write this book.

When not working on more Promised Land Diaries, Adams loves to read the classics and ancient history, taking many armchair travels in time to foreign lands. She especially loves reading biographies of famous authors.

She and her husband and their two children live in Phoenix, Arizona. They often hike in the mountainous desert surrounding their home and have been known to spot quail, coyote, an occasional fox, and many lizards. Not to be outdone by the great outdoors, they share their home with three dogs, a cat, and an assortment of little fish.

About the Illustrator

Dennis Edwards is the illustrator of three big Bible storybooks: *Heroes of the Bible, Boys Life Adventures,* and *My Bible Journey.* As a de-signer and illustrator, he's also contributed to numerous others.

His favorite books include Robert Louis Stevenson's *Treasure Island,* comic books, and science fiction–related books because "the sky's the limit," he always says.

Dennis also enjoys acting and at times gets to perform for the kids at his church.

He lives with his wife and son in West Chicago, Illinois.

Books in

Series

Coming in Summer 2004:

The author would like to thank Jerry Watkins, Todd Watkins and the staff of Educational Publishing Concepts. Jeanette Thomason for her excellent editorial guidance, the rest of the team of Baker Book House Company, as well as the talented Dennis Edwards and Donna Diamond.

Dedicated with love to my children Michal Tyra and Alexandra Tyra.

© 2004 by Baker Book House Company

Published by Baker Books
a division of Baker Book House Company
P.O. Box 6287, Grand Rapids, MI 49516-6287
www.bakerbooks.com

Printed in the United States of America

Library of Congress Cataloging-in-Publication Data is on file at the Library of Congress, Washington, D.C.

ISBN 0-8010-4524-X

Scripture is taken from the HOLY BIBLE, NEW INTERNATIONAL VERSION®. NIV®. Copyright © 1973, 1978, 1984 by International Bible Society. Used by permission of Zondervan. All rights reserved.

Series Creator: Jerry Watkins and Educational Publishing Concepts, with Anne Tyra Adams
Cover Illustrator: Donna Diamond
Designer and Illustrator: Dennis Edwards
Editors: Jeanette Thomason, Kelley Meyne

The biblical account of Deborah can be found in the Bible's Old Testament, Judges 4–5. While Persis's dairies and the epilogue are based on this and historical accounts, the character of Persis, her diaries, and some of the minor events described are works of fiction.